June 5, 2016

Dear Lily,

May you enjoy my second novel as much as you did reading my first, Goodnight Eleanor.

Thank you for supporting this independent author!

Margie Bayer

# The Killdeer Song

*DEDICATION*

This book is for my grandparents,
who lived, toiled and loved
on the unforgiving North Dakota plains.

## *EPIGRAPH*

"It is the ordinary woman who knows
something about love; the gorgeous
ones are too busy being gorgeous."

~~Katherine Hepburn~~

"Anyone can love a rose,
but it takes a great deal
to love a leaf. It's ordinary
to love the beautiful, but it's
beautiful to love the ordinary."

# TABLE OF CONTENTS

Copyright .................................................. iv
Dedication ................................................. v
Epigraph ................................................... vi
Chapter  1—The Dutiful Brother .............. 9
Chapter  2—Café Anna ........................... 13
Chapter  3—Once Upon a Sunday ........... 22
Chapter  4—Anna's Ark ......................... 28
Chapter  5—The Peace Treaty ................. 56
Chapter  6—The Song of Wine ................ 81
Chapter  7—Harvest Moon ...................... 85
Chapter  8—Author of Rumors ................ 111
Chapter  9—The Quiet Man .................... 120
Chapter 10—The Guest ........................... 132
Chapter 11—The Lamp Lighter ............... 154
Chapter 12—The Field of Stones ............. 165
Chapter 13—The Velvet Box ................... 176
Chapter 14—Harvest of a Fool ................ 186
Chapter 15—The Killdeers' Song ............ 230
Chapter 16—A Mother A Memory ........... 240
Chapter 17—The Quiet Symphony of Love  257
Note to the Reader ................................... 265
About the Author ................................... 266

# CHAPTER 1—THE DUTIFUL BROTHER

The light of another day broke from the horizon and inched its way across the rolling fields and to the doorway of the old cedar barn in Dusty, Washington.

Blood red. Why did the sky have to be red after last night?

Was there no escaping the memory of the night before? Why did nature have to paint more blood in the sky? Was his body still so fresh that it dripped down from the heavens, or from wherever he was?

Gareth McManus had been leaning against the east door of the barn for maybe an hour. When he awoke, he was in one corner of a stall, and his older sister Anna was asleep in thick straw in the other. Richard and Polly McManus had covered both of them with heavy blankets sometime during the night.

When their daughter finally exhausted herself from crying and collapsed in the corner, it was Gareth who stayed with her. Close to her was an empty bottle of blush wine. How ironic for one human to wallow in the liquid and hide from suffering caused by another human who died by the bottle.

It was said at the accident scene that the deceased reeked of alcohol, and it was doubtful if he ever saw the telephone pole.

Gareth remembered Anna telling him just hours before how she hated bachelor parties. She never did understand why men had to have those stupid things. Although he was seven years away from the drinking age himself, he had heard plenty of what went on during the last hours of a single man's life. Usually, everyone had a good time. Usually lots of guys got drunk and wondered the next morning if they did anything really stupid.

Anna's fiancé had stopped by the house on the way to his party. She pleaded and pleaded with him not to drink. He had promised her he wouldn't. Gareth had heard the groom-to-be make the empty promise to his sister while he sat quietly on the porch.

In a few days Anna was to walk up to the altar and swear to God and mankind that she would give her heart away to the man beside her. Instead, Gareth heard it crack, and the sting of wine seeped deep into the red muscle. He loved his sister and didn't understand how life could treat her this way. What had she ever done to deserve this?

Polly McManus made her way up to the barn and stood at the doorway next to her son. She brought with her an old green thermos full of coffee, two old cups, and a plate of breakfast kept warm under foil. Her mouth was tight, and worried eyes went past him as they looked further into the barn.

She asked, "Has she awakened at all?"

Gareth shook his head.

"Did she drink quite a bit?"

Gareth glanced at the empty bottle again that lay near his sister. He replied, "Oh yeah, but she shouldn't have too much of a hangover."

"Gareth, how can you say that? Just look at her!" Mrs. McManus twisted her hands helplessly.

Gareth sighed. "Mom, I'm not sure which happened, but either the wine turned into tears, or the wine came out with the tears. Either way, I'd say she dried her crying well."

His mother shook her head and murmured, "My poor baby. . . my poor baby. . . "

Gareth said, almost in a whisper, "Has anybody called here yet?"

"Well, Pastor Edwards and his wife called first thing this morning. Then dear Mrs. Krumbly called and said that the Ladies Auxiliary Club will be sending meals for a week, bless their hearts," Mrs. McManus sighed. "I should go back in and call some folks who may not have heard about it." She sighed again. "What am I going to do?
What *am* I going to do?"

"Mom. . ."

A small "hmm" escaped from Mrs. McManus.

Gareth recalled, "Last night she said something that I'll never forget."

Without looking at her son, she asked, "And what was that?"

"She said, 'Gareth, life is the windshield and I am the bug.'"

Mrs. McManus started crying and handed her son the coffee, the cups, and his breakfast, and abruptly left the barn. When he uncovered the scrambled eggs, bacon, and toast spread with Anna's raspberry jam, Anna stirred and opened her eyes, but her stare went beyond the open door. She then spoke, as she often did, in her own strange way.

"Forget conversing
Whisper softly, if you please
Where's the rest of me?
Oh, yes
The core of my being
Disappeared with the liquid
I permit myself to chastise a parched fool
Promising a debonair second self
Cool grapes deceived me
Softly singing on the rim
What shall we do with a drunken lady?
Don't ask for decisiveness nor coherence
Please, pass the coffee
My bosom buddy,
 my dutiful brother judges me not
Oh, Humpty Dumpty.
 I feel your pain.
Won't you put me together again?"

## CHAPTER 2—CAFÉ ANNA

*Seven Years Later*

Dusty. What a name for a town. Pastor James Michael Edwards shook his head at the sign as he passed.

On his return he would need to take that exit, follow his aunt and uncle's directions to their house, and unpack his belongings from the back of his truck. Two days from now he would give his first sermon in a little white church nearby.

James had passed the sign on purpose. His uncle had said that it would be worth his while to go a little out of his way and have a bite to eat at a place called Richard's Café in Colfax. He was dying for a cup of coffee, wanted something hot to eat, and desperately needed to stretch his stiff, sore body. But most of all, he wanted to see another human being. Life as he knew it back in Seattle had no lack of humans at seven o'clock in the morning. Where were they in this miserable, cold, boring looking place called Eastern, Washington?

In the first few hours after heading out of Seattle, the young pastor was glad to be leaving his old life behind and anxious to start anew. But as the miles and the hours added up on that first Friday of January, James slowly began emerging from the fog in which he had preferred to exist for many months.

He had been staring at nothing for hours. All around him was nothing—hours and hours of nothing. His hands tightened around the steering wheel. Reality was hitting hard. He wished his head didn't hurt, he wished he wasn't tired and hungry, and he wished that he was back in his apartment. However, his apartment, his piano, and all of his furnishings had been left behind, under the care of a good friend, who had move in right away.

He remembered stuffing his belongings into boxes, and with that task done, the only thing left to do was go to sleep and wait for morning. He tried to sleep, but couldn't. As he paced the floor and stared out his window at the city lights, he knew what he had to do.

James chose to leave at a horrible time in the morning on purpose. He had to. If he waited to leave Seattle in the daylight, James did not think he could have pried himself away from the only life and city he knew.

And so, shortly after two in the morning, a man in his truck turned onto I-90 and headed east. The snowy conditions over the mountain pass kept him alert and distracted his mind from the reason he was leaving. He passed the towns of Cle Elum and Ellensburg, and as he closed in on Vantage, he checked his map with his flashlight and saw that he needed to leave I-90 and take Highway 26.

Keeping one eye on the road, James snuck a peek at the map again and noticed that he was halfway across the state. While stopping at Royal City for gas at $1.14 a gallon and a cup of mediocre coffee, he took a moment to read the letter from his aunt and uncle again.

*August 31, 1990*

*Dear James,*

*It was so good hearing from you a few weeks ago. Aren't telephones wonderful! You sounded as if you were just in the other room, instead of clear across the state.*

*We are terribly sorry to hear that your engagement has been called off. Thank you for sharing your heartache and sorrow with us. Both of us will be praying for you in hopes that you take refuge in the Lord and place your trust in Him.*

*As you know, dear nephew, your Auntie and I have been planning to take that Ireland vacation after we retire someday. Well, we're not sure if we are ready to officially retire, but we do know that Ireland is calling us. For sometime now we have been corresponding with long time friends who moved there a few years ago, and they would like us to stay with them for a while. They tell us that there is a little cottage close to their place in the country that is for rent. Who knows how long we'll stay. Six months, a year, two years? I suppose it would all depend upon our health, which is fairly good right now.*

*(Your Auntie is reminding me to write this right now because it is the main reason for this letter.)*

*That night after we spoke to you, we lay in bed and couldn't sleep. All we could think about was you and your broken heart, and us planning on leaving for Ireland sometime before we get too old for sightseeing. Your Auntie insisted that we get down on our knees and put our confidence and faith in the Lord; that He would give you strength, and for us, that He send a pastor who would look after our little flock with as much care and love as we have.*

*Just after we gave our troubles to God to solve, I looked at your Auntie, and she looked at me. I am holding my breath as I dare to even mention this to you. We know that Seattle has been the only life you have known, but we are wondering if you would like a change of pace. We would be honored if you could take over for us until we come back.*

*Please give this some serious consideration as we await your reply.*

*As always, you are forever in our thoughts and prayers.*

*Love Always,*
*Your Auntie and Uncle*

James leaned his head back and let out a groan. He closed his eyes for a moment and then forced them open again. He brought the coffee carefully to his lips, but it was still too hot. While it cooled off in a holder, James put the letter back in the envelope and tucked it under

16

another letter that gave the directions to his aunt and uncle's house. When James arrived there after his breakfast at Richard's Café, he would find it empty, for its owners had already left two days earlier. His aunt and uncle had wasted no time in leaving for the little cottage in Ireland.

Highway 26 took him past Othello, and then he continued about an hour on the straightest road he had ever traveled. He passed Palouse Falls, Hooper, Pampa, LaCrosse, Dusty, Mockonema, until he finally he saw the sign that indicated that breakfast was not far away.

Pastor James Edwards turned the steering wheel to the right, and having departed from Highway 26, he had arrived in Colfax. Almost to his destination, he sighed deeply at the thought of nearing the end of his 255-mile journey.

It was evident by the full parking lot in front that the little café was home to many morning people, so he pulled into a spot further down the street just a little after seven o'clock. He read the painted words on the window: "Richard's Café, Est. 1953." Upon entering, he noted it was not a fancy place by any means, but the colors and style from the early '50s gave the place a homey, warm, and simple feel.

As he stood next to the door, he took off his coat and hung it on the stand while a few heads turned in his direction. James paid no attention to the stares that were fixed on him as he let his own eyes roam and spotted five stools at the counter. A stocky older man occupied the fourth seat so James took up the second one.

"Move on down next to Curly," a woman's voice

instructed him. A plain young woman wearing a waist apron with jeans, T-shirt, and white sneakers swooshed passed him from behind.

"I don't see anybody sitting here except me."

"They're reserved, now move yourself on down." She snapped her fingers loudly. "Move it!"

The entire café looked at James with curious and annoying glances. Feeling like a true newcomer, he slid off his stool and sat down again to the right of Curly. If he hadn't been so tired and hungry, he might have taken up an argument with her. But not now—all he wanted was hot coffee and a plate of something to eat.

The waitress, the only waitress managing the busy cafe, swished over to the counter and quickly filled mugs. His own mug was turned over as she filled Curly's, then his.

"Thanks, love," muttered Curly.

"You bet," she threw back over her shoulder as she wiped the counter.

James was staring at her blankly, still somewhere in the realm of sleep.

"What's the matter now?" The waitress inquired with another look of annoyance.

James remarked, "Nothing, but aren't you supposed to find out if a customer wants some first?" Even though he welcomed the brew that sat in front of him, he found himself questioning her in a slightly sarcastic tone of voice.

The waitress stood there staring at him with one hand on her hip.

"No. Everyone here drinks coffee. If you don't want it, don't drink it!" she barked back, and with that she was gone.

Now this man Curly, who sat to the left of James, appeared to be in his late seventies, had short white hair that was flat on top and wore thick eyeglasses. Under his white T-shirt, James could see Navy tattoos.

James rested his arms on the counter, and lightly touching the hot mug with the palms of his hands asked, "Is what's-her-name always like that?"

"Like what, son?"

"Like—bitchy."

Curly turned to him and gave James a hard look through his thick glasses.

"Son, if I were you, I'd watch what you say 'round here. First, Anna ain't bitchy. That's just Anna. Second, if she heard you say that, well, your ass would have been thrown out."

He jerked his left thumb over his shoulder as he continued, "*And*, if she was really mad after that, she might throw the rest of us out, too!" Curly made a strange shivering noise as he shook his head. "Don't wanna rememba that time."

"That time? You mean she's done it before?" asked James, intrigued.

"Oh, yeah! Somebody pissed her off *real* good. The nincompoop said something 'bout her having PSM or PMS, or whateva it's called. First she kicked his ass out, then the whole bunch of us!"

Curly shook his head again, lamenting over his memory of the event. While he had been giving James a personality briefing of their waitress, Anna had placed three plates filled with eggs, bacon, toast, and pancakes on the counter, and quickly poured three coffees. James leaned forward slightly. He was puzzled, but the little café then got a wake-up call. Three men opened the door and took *their* places on *their* stools. They were quite boisterous—in a good-natured way. They greeted Curly, and lingering on the newcomer briefly, they nodded to James. James nodded back.

Anna finally took his order of pancakes and a side of bacon, shoved the white paper on the cook's spinning wheel, hit the chrome bell and shouted, "Seven-fifteen and all's well!"

James glanced around at the unfazed crowd. There was a growing wave of excitement throughout the cafe as voices rose, silverware chimed against plates, and glasses clinked in good cheer.

Anna cleared and set up tables, took money at the till, and flew here and there at a variety of tasks. Curly sat contentedly with his thick hands around his coffee cup, watching her work with a little smile on his face.

"She reminds me of my late wife, Blanche, God rest her soul," he remarked.

Having already placed a fork full of pancake in his mouth, James could only mumble, "I'm sorry."

"It's all right," Curly nodded. "It was her time to go, just as mine will be someday. Anyway, Blanche waitressed for years in Santa Rosa. She was the best there was. Anna reminds me so much of her." He paused for a moment. "See how she carries herself in this rush? Blanche called it *rhythm*. Anna doesn't make jerky movements. She makes every step, every turn looks almost like a dance step. You just watch her."

The young man had been watching her all the while before Curly mentioned it.

He continued, "She's always switching the guy's hats from one head to another, often wearing one 'til the customer has to go. She always asks them if they have a new joke to tell. If you can't think of one, she won't give you coffee. The guys love it 'cause everyone needs their coffee. The men bring in homemade bread, jams, and other goodies from their wives. Anna makes a special point to find out birthdays and puts balloons on the backs of chairs, and puts candles in muffins or on stacks of pancakes. Then she makes the bunch of us sing while we raise a toast with our coffee. The men call her a doll and a gem of a kid."

Curly poked a thick finger at James. "But, whateva you do, don't piss her off or you'll find your ass out the door!"

James washed the last of his breakfast down with coffee. As he slid off the stool and reached for his wallet in the back pocket of his jeans, he noticed that Anna was putting someone's hat on her head.

"Curly, it was nice meeting you."

The older man nodded.

"I've just got one thing to say. Are you sure this place isn't called *Café Anna*?"

## CHAPTER 3—ONCE UPON A SUNDAY

The door that separated him from the small congregation was closed. Until now, he always took those rectangular things that hung on hinges for granted. James blessed it for the moment, but cursed the ticking of his wristwatch that was louder than he ever remembered it sounding.

He stood alone in the vestibule, asking himself why he ever wanted to be a pastor in the first place. It certainly wasn't to see how badly his hands would shake on his first Sunday. His hands were lifted in front of him. They were cold, clammy, and trembled slightly on their own. They turned over a few times, showing the new pastor different roads which could be traveled. James wished one of them would lead him away from the little white church.

Suddenly he jumped when the organist began playing *How Great Thou Art*.

"You're helping a lot!" he accused the woman in

the other room.

Turning towards the hanging vestments, he removed a white one from the plastic hanger and slipped it over his head. At least, it was supposed to go over his head. There was a knock at the door and a woman's voice asked, "Pastor Edwards, are you in here?"

He had to laugh at himself for the sight he must have offered her.

"Here, let me help you with the zipper. Bend your knees a bit. There."

A small-framed woman in her late sixties to early seventies smiled warmly up at him as she said, "Good Morning! Just wanted to see how things are."

"Could be better."

"I'm Mrs. Krumbly."

"And I'm the nervous pastor."

He held out his hands and the older woman held them in her warm, steady ones. She smiled. "It's to be expected. Never saw a pastor who hasn't felt what you're feeling now." She shrugged slightly. "Call it the inevitable. Don't dwell on it, and before you know it, it will be over."

Mrs. Krumbly patted his hands and then left to join the congregation. James noticed she closed the door only halfway, perhaps as an invitation to follow.

The sound of the organ died away, and James placed a hand on the glass doorknob, pausing long enough to feel its cool, smooth surface. Words of advice from his uncle suddenly floated to the surface of his memory.

"Fear must be looked straight in the eye. It can eat you up, or you can face it. One way or the other, the feelings are going to be there. It is how you handle the situation that will determine the growth or lack of growth within your character. Just remember, James, in life you choose your character—it doesn't choose you."

Straightening his back, he closed the door to his comfort zone room gently behind him and took his place at the wooden pulpit.

"Good Morning," he timidly greeted the strangers below him.

"Good Morning!" they joyfully shouted back.

Pastor James Edwards jumped in slight exaggeration that brought a smile to his face and on the faces of his little flock before him. Everyone had a good laugh while the ice melted, and he was glad he hadn't taken a road away from his little church. His. James smiled at the realization that it was his—for a while. It was the first time in his life he had something to call his own, and it felt good.

Sitting next to her husband, six pews back on the left side of the church, was the friendly face of Mrs. Krumbly. Her soft smile and reassuring warm eyes told him, "See, everything's okay." He nodded to her, and clearing his voice, he began talking about how privileged he was to begin his pastoral life in their church.

His eyes were saying hello to the sea of faces below, when to his right, in the third pew from the front, a newly familiar face stood out. He found himself locking eyes with the young woman, although not intentionally. But there she was, in his church, sitting there with her arms crossed, and a look set upon her face that plainly spoke for her.

It was odd that he felt so much dislike towards a person whom he had had the displeasure of meeting just two days before. It was rare for Pastor James Edwards to not get along with the human race. To his knowledge, she may have been only the second individual, after his mother, whom he truly disliked.

He had met Anna on her turf; and now she was on his. James stood there glaring at her, almost absentmindedly, and oblivious to those around him. His face began to grow warm and hot prickles crawled over the skin on the back of his neck. He imagined his ears were bright red, as they also felt warm. She was beginning to rattle his composure and confidence, yet she wasn't doing anything as obnoxious as hitting the stupid chrome bell at the café. Nor was she running around from pew to pew swapping hats from a few elderly men who held them securely on their laps. So why was she throwing him off balance so easily? It took more than a crude stare to shake him. Her presence to him was like listening to someone just learning to play a musical instrument and not being able to get away from it.

*Clear your voice and look away*, he told himself. *Just look away!* He broke eye contact with her and quickly noticed that other eyes in the room had an interest in them. It was in his best interest to quickly get on with things. James continued talking about himself, which led up to the present time. The congregation listened intently, smiled, and laughed at his humor.

Everyone did, that is, except *her*. In the third pew sat *that* person. The waitress. Her. She was in the company of a family who he assumed were her parents, brothers, and sisters. James tried to ignore the young woman who looked to be close to his thirty years of age. But to ignore her would be ignoring others around her. He knew first impressions were important, but maybe he could shift his eyes to the left of the church for a moment, and then try again. Before his eyes got a chance to shift left, a movement caught his attention.

*She* was gently rocking in the pew, leaning her head to one side, eyes closed, a smile slapped on her lightly freckled face.

*Oh, Lord Jesus. What the hell is she doing?* James groaned silently.

The parishioners around her didn't seem distracted in the least, but James had had enough. He walked down to the right side of the church and rested his hands on the first pew. It became evident to the family that Anna sat with that Pastor Edwards was addressing her, as he stood there with eyes firm upon her as he continued speaking. The assumed siblings that sat on either side of her tried to bring her back from wherever she was. Perhaps his uncle was used to her odd behavior, but James wasn't going to stand for it. She was not going to upset his first sermon in the little white church that was going to be his until his auntie and uncle returned.

A young man had given her arm a good yank.

"What?" she loudly snapped.

Her eyes quickly opened and darted to the young man then to the pastor. James found himself stopping in mid-sentence, and never in his life had he witnessed such silent anger in a human being.

Then, in the horribly dead-silent room, a lone fly made a pinging noise against the stained glass window. Its high-pitched buzzing filled the voiceless room while the dumb insect buried itself in a corner.

And then she rose, ever so slowly, with purpose, placing her hands on the back of the pew before her. She was not tall, but every inch of her stretched above the crowd as if someone were pulling her hair from above. Without permission, a shiver ran up his back and James wondered if he should be afraid. He held his ground. He heard his voice say something about a song and number 114 and having everyone stand. Turning towards the altar, James went up the two steps, and the only sound in the little church was that of the fly trying to escape the colored glass. James took his place at the wooden pulpit, and opening the songbook, he began to drown out the fly. Hesitantly, other voices joined his.

But the door at the back of his little church slammed shut, echoing loudly. The startled people half-ceased in their singing. Their faces followed the echo that began at the door and ended at the pulpit. James did not allow his eyes to leave the songbook. They remained safely on the printed pages. Although he could not directly see them, he felt many eyes casting up judgment upon him, probably even from Mrs. Krumbly.

It was then that he noticed the fly. *It* had landed on his songbook. *It* sat there with ugly eyes and James was sure it was staring at him. The two halves of the songbook slammed together, and somewhere between the pages was the dead fly.

## CHAPTER 4—ANNA'S ARK

The kitchen was quiet, as it ought to be for a non-morning person. Mornings were something that had to be dealt with delicately. The warm cup of black coffee that both hands held up to his mouth helped ease James into the first Saturday of March.

Sitting at the little table against the south window, his crossed bare feet touched the cold linoleum floor, and although one side of his brain told him to put on a pair of socks, the other part was still in a state of half-slumber, and so James sat in his long pajama pants waiting for the coffee to take effect.

Gradually his eyes managed to focus past the curtains, through the window glass, over the lawn, and out to the fields where they settled on his neighbor's barricade of trees, acres and acres away. The uneven few inches of dim light that hid behind the distant poplar trees appeared as a striking silhouette cut out on black paper and glued to the imaginary horizon.

Another dawn was unfolding itself and the waking occupant at the table ran his fingers through his untidy medium-dark blond hair. James thought about dropping a few slices of bread in the toaster, but sighed out loud at the notion of crossing the cold floor. His feet had warmed themselves and would be safe as long as he didn't move them.

He turned his attention back to the window, and let his eyes glide to the morning sky. Above the depressing color of dull light, a fuzzy grayness filtered down like the edges of a cotton ball into the bit of daybreak. As far as his eyes were permitted to wander, the world outside was a vast sea of gray, and the promise of rain was not so much a threat but a promise. It was only a matter of time before the merciless skies opened and the damp air would be filled with cold, driving rain.

And if nature wasn't depressing enough, James felt a numbing thought inch its way through his brain. The coffee had done its job too well. He covered his face with his hands and let the weight of his head fall into them. He groaned and muttered, "damn," which fell on the deaf ears of the kitchen walls. In the darkness that his hands provided, her face emerged through the murky waters of memory. There she stood, again, her face frozen in anger, a fire that showed she despised him set in her eyes.

James let his hands slide through his hair again, but this time his head felt heavier on his shoulders.

His stomach begged for nutrition but he ignored it. He sat in the quiet kitchen, his calculating mind trying to work out a plan of action to detain his duty. Any deceptive scheme or maneuver would do. But what?

He shook his head in defeat. The kitchen clock glared at him and nagged him, and in return he glared back, but he heard the cry of procrastination.

He left the kitchen, took a shower, dressed in jeans and T-shirt, grabbed his truck keys and coat, and tried to leave his attitude behind the front door. The front door slammed anyway.

Dark gray skies hung above acres of McManus land—over a thousand acres, he had been told. James drove somewhat more slowly than usual over the rolling land. He really didn't have to be doing this, he told himself over and over.

After last Sunday's service, Anna's younger brother Gareth paid him a visit in the vestibule. He wasted no time, nor did he mince words while explaining to the new pastor that he was very close to his sister and looked after her. Gareth strongly recommended patching things up with her. He wasn't asking for an apology because he himself had to admit that Anna had a way of trying one's patience.

"Somehow, some way, if you can set things right between the two of you, maybe she'll come back to church." As Gareth departed, he added, "You don't have to like her or understand her. Just try. . .to get along with her."

James thought it was interesting that Gareth was so protective of a sister who didn't seem to need his protection. From what he saw, Anna appeared resourceful with her temper and did not need reinforcement from family members.

His truck turned into the long driveway, and as he neared the dwellings where the family lived, huge walnut trees hung their bare branches over the driveway as if they were escorting him for his own protection.

A two-story house sat off to his left and the white smoke from the chimney waved in greeting. The wooden barn that loomed in front of him dwarfed the McManus home and could have been mistaken for an ark. He slowed down and came to rest just past the walkway near a garage. He turned the keys toward him and the truck fell silent.

James Edwards did not want to be there. He wanted to be back home, in his pajamas, and reading the morning paper in his favorite sofa chair while enjoying a cup of coffee. But as he sat in his truck, a cold March morning shiver took him by surprise. He brought his arms closer to his body. His skin shook again and a visible huff of annoyance filled the chilly air.

It was not in his nature to apologize to people. James Edwards by nature was rarely wrong, and having to smooth this situation over pained him greatly. But the new pastor knew that if he didn't at least speak to the guilty party, his career at the little church might just as well be over.

His feet carried him down a narrow cement path, under a large leafless grape arbor and past a small pump house that greeted him with a constant humming sound. To the right of the naked arbor was a large rectangle of split cedar fencing that incased a few battered but standing corn stalks from the previous summer.

Emerging from the arbor was another walkway running the length of the farmhouse. Ahead of him was a cement rise that could put him at the door in a moment, but he noticed that to his left there were white pillars on the end of the house. He had not paid attention to them while driving up and could only guess they were part of a porch. Not that a damn porch mattered to him, because it didn't.

For a moment he stood, letting out one last but necessary sigh, then placed himself upon the step and made a loose fist. Knocking on the front door a few times, he was warmly greeted by Mrs. McManus, who insisted immediately that he should call her Polly.

"I've been expecting you," she said, smiling.

"You have?" James asked, puzzled.

"Well, I've been hoping you would come. My son Gareth told me that he spoke to you, and well, I don't know what he said, but Gareth can be a bit too persuasive at times."

James thought back on the conversation her son had had with him. Come to think of it, James had not been able to utter one word in his defense.

"Not at all, ma'am," he lied.

"Well, you're here, and that's all that matters now. Please, come in Pastor Edwards."

Once inside, he found himself in the family room that was heated by a woodstove nestled in a corner. Older pieces of furniture wrapped around the brick hearth; a few could have been heirlooms from past generations. Above the sofa, a wall was smothered in framed photographs.

A smiling little girl caught his eye. Her hair was cut in a boy's style, freckles could have been mistaken for a pair of glasses, and half of a front tooth was missing. The very plain girl—to put it politely—could have been any one of the sisters, but the girl in the photo proudly held a violin in her arms.

He noticed that Mrs. McManus was waiting for him, and as he started to follow her to the kitchen, a china hutch caught his attention and he stopped to study the collection of nice pieces.

She explained, "We received a few tea cups and saucers as wedding gifts, and every year after that I've been collecting them from Germany, Ireland, Scotland, and Great Britain, which is my ancestry." She laughed as she added, "And I don't have to tell you that 'McManus' is Irish!"

She explained that her husband was in town running errands and the kids were scattered here and there. He was asked to sit down at the table so she could talk to him before he went out to the barn where Anna was.

As he settled himself down at the large rectangular table, he immediately caught sight of a thermos and two coffee cups sitting on the counter. He turned and glanced at Anna's mother, gave the articles another scrutinizing glance, and finally settled his smiling eyes back at the woman who in turn smiled at him.

"But you didn't know I was coming," he said, puzzled.

"True. But when I did catch sight of you, that truck of yours was taking its time coming up that long driveway. So you see, you gave me plenty of time to get things ready."

James paused, then he grinned and nodded his head slowly.

"Yes ma'am," he admitted, and a chuckle escaped after he imagined how ridiculous he must have appeared.

A moment or two passed and Mrs. McManus took in a breath and let it out with a sigh. "I saw you looking at Anna's picture in the family room. Spunky little thing she was. Seemed like she was always laughing. . ." Mrs. McManus stopped. "I haven't heard my daughter laugh, well, let's just say it's been a long, long time, and I miss hearing it."

She placed her hands out in front of her on the table, right hand over the left, smoothing the bottom one as if to make the veins and wrinkles go away. But James saw that her face was content with what she saw and felt. While raising a large family and laboring day after day ever since she had said "I do," perhaps she regarded them a symbol of her life; as a farm wife, as a mother, as a woman. Her life was there for him to see, and James saw that she was both proud and wise, and nothing was going to take that away from her.

Her voice slowly filled his ears and he brought his mind back into the conversation.

"Sometimes, I almost forget what it used to sound like. Sometimes I think she was *liked* just on account of her wonderful laugh."

Mrs. McManus' soft lines about her face grew firmer as she spoke; she folded her arms under her chest, and her hazel-gray eyes glared at the table. They were darkened by sadness over a memory that was only known to those who knew her daughter.

James moved slightly in his seat as if that would ease the awkward, heavy silence that was unintentionally created; but created nonetheless. He carefully cleared his throat, and backing his chair slowly away from the table of gloom, he quietly suggested, "Perhaps I should go to the barn now."

"Oh—I am sorry. Please forgive me. Don't know what came over me," she sighed. "Yes, that would be good."

He rose from his chair, relieved.

Mrs. McManus went to the counter where the coffee and cups had patiently been waiting, and handed them to the young pastor, who had slowly made his way to the kitchen door. The scratched and worn greenish-gray thermos was tucked under his left arm while two old coffee cups clanked against each other as his long forefinger tightened around the handles.

"Now you just head up to the knoll there, see, past the white corkscrew lilac tree—well, it will be white soon—past the garden, through the wooden gate, and then enter the barn to the east."

She stood next to the kitchen door and held it open as James paused on the threshold. She placed her other hand upon his left arm, a mother's caring and knowing hand. Her wise, gentle eyes met his as she detained his mission for a moment.

"On Anna's behalf, and for her own sake, *please* do not give up." Her voice was slightly firm, but in no manner unkind. "No matter what she says or does, do not give up. Please."

The young pastor felt her eyes pleading with him as if he were God himself. The pressure increased on his arm to match the sincerity of her plea.

"I'll see what I can do."

Mrs. McManus gently released him, smoothed his coat sleeve, and raised the corners of her mouth to form a small grin.

"Thank you."

As he gathered the mugs and the thermos, he wanted to tell her that if his mission failed it was not his fault. Having been given the title of "Pastor" did not give him powers to right all wrongs. Saying, "I'll see what I can do", was not a promise of any sort, and did not guarantee instant success in resolving matters that may have occurred years ago.

He was not a psychiatrist by profession and wanted no part of it. Although, in just two months as pastor of the little white church, he discovered on his weekly visits with folks that they would ask him questions that would better have been asked in a psychiatrist's office.

He could only match Mrs. McManus' feeble smile with one of his own. Nodding to her, James turned and made his way passed the tree that he was assured would bloom with white flowers soon. Leaning his body slightly forward he ascended the knoll. As he placed one foot in front of the other, a gut feeling told him that this mother regarded *this* daughter similarly to her fine bone china.

"Mother's blood by way of Germany, Scotland, Ireland, and Great Britain. Father's blood by way of Ireland," he mumbled. James wanted to spit on the ground but thought it best not to, just in case Mrs. McManus was watching.

"Fragile my ass!" he muttered.

Gradually, as he neared the top of the knoll he thought he heard what sounded like the strings of a bow press against wires of a violin. His feet stopped and he listened. It came from within the large structure that loomed before him. The sounds were beautiful as he pictured the bow caressing its cousin the strings. The music was fragile, delicate, shy, yet strong.

This beautiful music could not be coming from the same person whom he met at Richard's Café. There was no way that what he was hearing could come from the same person who slammed the church door. This music was real and required a human with a soul and heart that was sensitive and had feelings. This was not possible, for James was clearly convinced that Anna McManus was far from human and couldn't possess such characteristics. And while he stuck to his convictions, musical notes filled his head.

James had taken up the piano not long after he turned thirteen. His uncle played the piano so it didn't seem such an odd thing for him to do. His mother wanted to buy a baby grand for him so he could practice at home with an instructor under her scrutiny, but the whole idea was to spend more time *away* from her. Her wings would have suffocated and snuffed out any flames of interest had James let her get her way.

She'd wailed to her husband at the dinner table one night, "A piano would look so stunning, so showy in the front room! Our friends would be jealous knowing we have a pianist in the family. Can't you just see a cute little black one over there? Or do I want a white one? I could have the ladies over for coffee. Oh, then I would have to buy new china. I think I saw in Sunday's paper that Frederick & Nelson is having a sale. . ."

Her mouth had not stopped moving and the gush of words that filled her ears had only added more fuel to her tongue. James wanted to aim a fork full of mash potatoes at her forehead; better yet in her mouth, not that it would have helped any. He couldn't stand it any longer and filled his fork with ammunition and was ready to launch its target, but his father shook his head and James shoved the ammunition in his own mouth.

His father had grinned and then winked at him. In the end, James rode the bus once a week to his instructor until he graduated from Franklin High School. He received a full scholarship to the University of Washington, majoring in music. But after a short and unfulfilling career, he had chosen to follow in his uncle's footsteps.

His own footsteps moved forward to the wooden gate next to the barn. Rearranging things under his arm, he turned the cold steel latch, walked through the gate, and replaced the latch again. Next to his feet the mud was fresh except nearest to the barn wall where it was powder dry. Staying close to the weather-beaten east wall, he stepped inside the dark room.

It was long and narrow, and due to the gray skies dwelling outside, the only light that came in was through the open door and two small, dusty, thin, windows—one on each side of the door. In front of him were two open stalls with troughs at the front. Above him the music floated and lingered upon his wakening senses. His eyes that were focusing in the interior dusk had never seen such so much solid cedar. Everything about the barn exemplified outstanding workmanship. The uneven, smooth cedar planks under him, the cedar walls, the round, smooth, shiny beams that he could not resist touching, were all as solid as solid could be.

Her music stopped for a moment, and then continued. Perhaps it was the sweetness of the hay, decades of animals living and breathing in the old barn, the old wood, birds from somewhere within the barn talking to each other; he couldn't just say, but listening, inhaling, and touching his surroundings stirred a new sensation within him. James would have liked to have had listened to more of her music, but he was not there for his own pleasure.

On the other side of the stall troughs was a very narrow and dark passageway. Placing his left hand on the smooth wood, he began moving forward one step at a time. Touching the stall divider, he held onto the next trough rail on the opposite side. To his right and ahead a bit was an open doorway, but somewhere below was an unseen step, and thumping into it, he plunged forward, hitting his knee in the fall. He swore countless times in his head as a sharp pain shot through his leg while a voice from the rafters demanded, "Who's there?"

James managed to cease his swearing. Realizing he dropped the thermos and cups in the fall, he reluctantly put a hand on the landing to search for them. Fortunately, for his imagination that didn't need feeding, there were no barn dwellers to meet his fingers. He held onto the door jamb and pulled himself up, then limped into the large room. Slowly turning, he saw stacks of hay to his right that looked like a stairway leading to the ceiling, but they leveled off at the rafters. His eyes and body continued turning to the right, to a floor above him which probably was the ceiling to the room he had departed. One last turn put him facing east, a pair of legs dangling off the upper floor catching his attention. As his eyes rose, he saw the violin resting on her lap, and at last his eyes rested upon her face. James could not decide which was colder; the chilly air or her stare.

"Good morning," he said reluctantly.

Anna did not reply.

"I heard you playing. . ." he began, but his words suddenly crumbled.

Anna took up her violin and embraced it against her chest. Her deep stare cut him off, and while she said nothing, her eyes latched onto his in a way that was more than slightly intimidating.

"You're awfully quiet when you're not banging church doors."

She surprised him by her silence even after he provoked her.

He cleared his throat. "You could tell me that my presence is about as welcome as a flea on a dog."

Still, she remained silent.

He cleared his throat again and mockingly said, "Well, this is going better than I expected."

Anna then picked herself off the hay-covered rafter, turned her back to him and placed the violin and bow back in its case.

"I was hoping I could talk to you," James blurted out when he saw that her feet were carrying her across the rafter floor and towards the pyramid of hay bales.

A trickle of desperation flowed inside him, and upon his arm he could feel Mrs. McManus' strong fingers.

"Please stay—there is something that I have to say to you," he implored.

To his surprise she stopped and glared at him from

high above.

"Have to? Are you implying that there is no genuine sincerity attached to the words that are lying and waiting on your tongue, whatever they may be, Mr. Edwards? Perhaps a person such as yourself has deleted such words as need to, would like to, and, last but not least, *should*, from your vocabulary, finding them unnecessary, or perhaps beneath you?"

He could have convinced himself that her clawing remarks did not and could not affect him. His outgoing personality, charisma, and good looks had always served as a shield, his armor against rejection in his life. No one had ever challenged what lay hidden under that armor—until now.

He began once more by taking a deep breath. Letting it out slowly, he cleared his throat.

"Miss McManus, there is something. . ." James cleared his throat again, "that I wish to speak to you about."

The young woman who stood on top of the bales of hay slowly shook her head at him.

"My God! That must have hurt!"

It took all his strength to keep his teeth together and keep his feet from leaving the cold, dark barn. Besides his mother, no other female had *ever* verbally assaulted him in his life.

He stood there, equally dumbfounded and angry. Part of him wanted to go to where she stood, throw her damn violin across the barn in hopes of it crashing against the floor in pieces, and after watching it break, he would smile and then grab her by the shoulders and shake her. And although the thought swiftly raced through his mind, James was not a man who carried out such violent acts upon another human being. But even after the thought was dismissed, it bothered him that he, as a pastor, should even harbor such images, even for a moment.

As he stood there on the cedar planks, he eyed the door that brought him into the huge room. His mind was walking out the door, out of the barn, and his truck was leaving McManus soil. He would make sure that the thermos and cups were set down. James at least had enough respect for Mrs. McManus and would feel that he had failed in *her* eyes. Other than that, he was beginning to not give a darn about Anna McManus, and wanted *her* to apologize to him for having wasted his morning. James Edwards never lost at anything, and to walk away from this would be a first. His eyes turned towards her and narrowed sharply.

"If I may, I would just like to say that you are the biggest pain in the ass I've had the misfortune of knowing."

"Correction. The misfortune is mine. But I didn't know that pastors were allowed to use such language. Could this be the nasty, undesirable side of your personality that nobody gets to see—except God and me? I wonder what He thinks about you *now*?"

"I'm sure He agrees with *my* opinion regarding *you*."

She looked at him for a moment or two, and then a little grin grew on her face. Anna let out a chuckle. "Despite what I think of you, I could say that I find you amusing—if I wanted to."

"So, why don't you?"

Her eyes narrowed slightly and the grin relaxed while she contemplated whether to answer him or not.

"All right, I will. Despite what I *think* of you, I do find you amusing. But, I only say that because, there aren't very many people who can amuse me anymore."

"Well, thank you, I think."

Their breath was visible and hung momentarily in the air while each studied the other from a distance. The thick fog of tension that separated them seemed to dissipate. James thought the waters of communication were warming; the deep waters were becoming shallow and therefore safe to walk in.

He started, "I would like to apologize for. . ."

"An apology?" A quick laugh descended upon him. "So *this* is what your little visit is all about. I suppose, considering what you're holding in your hands, that this wasn't *your* idea." Anna paused. "Was it?" An even more uncomfortable pause followed.

"Tell me, Mr. Edwards, that you have come here on your *own* free will. That this was *your* idea, and *yours* alone. Please tell me Mr. Edwards, because I really need to know if there's a scrap of honest decency left in mankind. If there is, then I will ask God to forgive me for all the dirty, rotten things I've ever thought about you."

A wash of shame prickled his skin, and not too far away, a strange feeling roamed throughout his gut, forecasting a turn of events. He breathed in slowly to delay the inevitable accusations. Bending his head down, he let the air out.

"I *am* sorry. I should have apologized sooner for embarrassing you in church the way I did."

His words, riding on a moment of hope, became lifeless and deteriorated shortly after leaving his mouth. Anna's face was flushed with anger and disappointment, her chin lifted high. Within him, a long, deep cut began leaking humiliation, and the words she spoke were thrown at him like salt.

"My mother and brother Gareth talked to you. Didn't they? I know them *too* well. And though I love them dearly, they had no business doing what they did." She paused for a few moments. "So, Mr. Edwards, if they hadn't pleaded with you, would you have come?"

The silence came to rest on him, and her words became his burden.

"Would you have come, Mr. Edwards?" she asked again, only louder.

She stood there on top the bales like a frightening cement statue glaring down at him. "Would-you-have-come?" she shouted.

What could he say, except the truth, which was spoken by his silence?

"I didn't think so!"

She spat the words at him, then descended the bales slowly and stood beside him.

"You are no different from them. It doesn't matter that one is six feet under, another is guilty of a crime— yet never sentenced, and you—*you*. Men are. . .all the same."

James kept his head bent as he bore his punishment. She moved away from him, walking slowly as if she were not in a hurry to leave. But she walked as one whose spirit had been broken further; a soul that was reminded of dark hours. He saw her making her way toward the east door and something within him wanted to grab her and pull her back. Some horrible injustice had been done to her. Just what, he didn't know, but he was not a member of inhumanity.

"Damn it, woman!" he cried, his voice reaching to every corner of the barn, "doesn't saying 'I'm sorry' mean *anything* to you!?"

Anna stopped. Her shoulders drooped forward. Her head bent down as if it were a broken flower stem.

"Don't go," he begged, his voice not much above a whisper. "Don't go. . ."

To James' surprise and relief she gradually turned around, and across her face she wore the lines of grief— pains of the past, but pains not forgotten. Her downcast eyes seemed to lead her back to the bales of hay, and upon reaching them she sat down heavily, holding the violin case across her lap. James cautiously took up a seat on the adjoining bale, and putting the two cups down next to him, his cool hands opened the thermos top. The escaping steam quickly rose from the canister. Pouring the dark coffee into the old cups that seemed at home now, James held one out for her.

"No, thanks," she muttered quietly.

"Someone once told me that *everyone* drinks coffee around here," he gently reminded her.

Anna let out a small, half-laugh. "Someone, huh?"

"'fraid so."

Putting the violin case next to her, her hands reached out with some reluctance for the steaming liquid.

"Thanks," she said in a quiet voice, without making eye contact.

James likewise replied in a hair above a whisper,

"You're welcome," without making eye contact with Anna.

They sat without saying a word. He could hear her lips opening to ready themselves for a sip. He watched her breath escape from her mouth, pushing the thin steam away. She did not look at him for five, maybe seven minutes. But the silence was not a bad thing altogether.

Anna rose from her seat, and casually strolling to the south, she played with hay under her feet. She held her cup between her breasts as if to keep them warm, and all the while James kept his eyes on her. He studied her ordinary face, observed the way she carried herself in her jeans and the way she lifted her eyes to a place above them.

Suddenly she spoke. "In a corner, way up there, is a family of barn swallows. Every year they make new nests out of mud, straw, horsehair, feathers, and that kind of stuff. Usually just about anything will do if it will strengthen their home. When I'm out here after dusk, it's hard to tell them apart from bats. They come swooping through that little door up there in the pitch of the roof, or through the east door, or by way of the milk parlor doors over there," she added, nodding to the west.

James leaned forward and rested his elbows close to his knees while watching and listening to her explain "Barn Swallow Home Building 101." To another person, such talk might have put one's ears to sleep, but to the former city dweller, James found such facts interesting.

"No, I don't care too much for bats. Not that

they've done me any harm, but they just make me feel uneasy when I can't distinguish them from a swallow. I guess it didn't help my dislike for them after mom told us the story of her encounter with one."

She continued, "As the story goes, when she was very young, on one hot summer night she was taking a bath. Since it was so hot, the window was open and a little bat came flapping in. The darn thing landed right in her hair and got all tangled up. Grandpa and grandma came running in when they heard her yelling in fright, while the bat wasn't too excited being stuck in her hair either. They got it out eventually, but to this day I don't think mom cares too much for them. Like I say, I've never run into one and would like to keep it that way."

Turning his way, she looked slightly startled as if she had forgotten he was sharing her presence there.

"Here I am carrying on about bats and birds while I'm boring you to death."

"On the contrary."

His probing eyes remained fixed on her. It was his turn to amuse himself and he felt no obligation to make her feel comfortable. Anna lowered her eyes and turned away from him, sliding loose hay under her right foot.

At first, James was only watching her play with the straw, but his eyes became unfocused and he let his thoughts wander. The huge, dark, chilly barn felt as if it were planted in the middle of nowhere without a living thing around for thousands of miles.

In his mind, he stood in a field of wheat and saw only land and the heavens above it. His feet continued turning and turning, crushing the grain against the earth. His eyes searched in vain for a building, a tree, a bird, a human being. But as far as his eyes traveled, he only saw the golden land and the blue sky that hung above it. With each turn of his feet, the emptiness inside of him grew heavier. The earth, which could hold him no longer, opened herself up and claimed him for eternity.

His fingers nervously turned his coffee cup that was almost too cold to hold around in his hands. Setting the cup down on the bale, he hugged his body with crossed arms as the damp air had nestled under his coat and made his skin shiver. He wanted to ask her one question, but the words that waited on his tongue had doubts about its acceptance. James was not about to wait for an invitation from patience.

"May I ask you something?"

Anna turned and looked at him. Her eyes were hesitant and cautious.

"Depends."

"I was just wondering, if. . . if you've ever left this place?"

She began to go through the motions of crossing her arms under her breasts, but the cup in her hand muddled the effort so she held it close to her body. Anna tilted her head back and closed her eyes. Her thoughts moved across her face in a way that made him regret having asked.

"I didn't mean to offend—I just. . ."

Anna shook her head. "You have not, Mr. Edwards."

She turned and came back to him, climbing two bales behind him, settling on the tightly twined makeshift seats. James had to turn lengthwise on the bale so she wasn't looking at his backside.

"No, I have not. But I've often thought about

visiting the other side of the mountains."

"Why haven't you?" James asked politely.

She shrugged. "I don't know. I guess my life here keeps me kind of busy, and such thoughts have always remained, just that. Wishful thoughts."

Anna abruptly grabbed a piece of dry grass and yanked it out from under the twine. Tossing it aside, she peered into her cup. Unscrewing the thermos top, James reached out a hand and offered to take her cup, but since she was too far away from him, she moved down one bale and placed it in his hand. The steam from the hot coffee rose between them. He wasn't quite sure what made his eyes follow the waving steam, but he was still watching it as Anna took a sip. She licked her lips. James studied them. Her lips moved again as she said, "Thanks."

She leaned back and straightened her spine. The brief, unexpected pause of his attention on her lips disturbed him. And when he lifted his face, he found her eyes waiting for his. How many moments had he had kept her waiting? James tried to think. She took another sip and sighed deeply. He should not be thinking about her lips. After all, he did not like Anna McManus. He needed to remind himself of that. He had to keep talking. He cleared his throat.

"Where would one of those wishful places be that you think about, but haven't gone to?"

"The San Juan Islands. I've seen pictures of them and read about them," she confessed.

"So what's keeping you from going?"

Anna lowered her eyes. "Well, I'm kind of needed here, you know. Someone has to feed all those folks who come to the café. For quite a few, the café is their home. But even if I did want to go, who would take care of them? Nobody knows them like I do. They would miss me. So you see, I don't think I could go, because I am *needed* here."

"I see," James pondered. "Well, I think you'd change your mind, if you only knew how nice it really is there."

Upon hearing this Anna suddenly leaned forward and inquired with interest, "Have *you* been to any of the islands?"

James smiled in spite of himself. "Sure. Every summer my best friend and I fly to Blakely Island, where his folks own a cabin that looks out towards Orcas Island and Friday Harbor."

Intrigued, Anna questioned, "Who does the flying?"

"My friend does. He has a nice Mooney at Boeing Field."

"I bet it's a nice place."

"It is."

"What is the Island like?"

"Well." James had to pause for a moment or two. "The fishing is great."

Anna shook her head at him.

"What? I said that the fishing is great."

"That's fine, but what is the island *like*?"

James looked at Anna, who was leaning toward him with eagerness and determination written across her face, waiting for the right answer.

"What is it like?" he repeated. "It's a little piece of land surrounded by water."

Anna planted her face in her hands.

"What? Don't you like my answer? Other than great fishing, that's as good as it gets."

"Typical," she lamented. "And don't try to apologize. I'm afraid you're just one of those folks who can only see trees in a forest but not notice the life that is scurrying around you."

James sat there staring at this person perched above him with the sincerest air about her.

"Typical?"

"Shh. . ."

"Apologize?"

"Shh. . ."

"What can't I see?"

"Hush."

He began to open his mouth, but she was quick to raise her eyebrows and one finger. James released a deep sigh, shut his mouth, and succumbed to her hushing and shushing. She set her coffee down and descended to his level, never taking her eyes off him.

Anna settled on the makeshift chair with her right leg under her and the other touching the floor. James wondered if she was aware of just how close she was to him. But how could she place herself so close to him while having declared her dislike for him? Anna was sitting *too* close. Even though he did not care for her, strange and interesting feelings did not go unnoticed.

"Now," she quietly instructed James, "close your eyes and take your body, your mind, and your soul to the island."

He reluctantly shut his eyes and sighed heavily.

"This isn't working."

"Just give it a try," she implored. "Now, where are you?"

"In your barn."

He opened his eyes to see her hands reaching for his face.

Leaning back a little she gently ordered, "Come here." Once again she reached out for his face and placed her hands on his cheeks. "Now," Anna began, the tone of her voice slightly demanding yet gentle, "Take your whole being to the lake where the fishing is great. You are there alone. What do you see?"

What did he see? This woman, whom he had mildly disliked from the first day he drove into Colfax, was alone with him, her hands were holding him, and she wanted him to go elsewhere.

"It would help if you closed your eyes," she suggested.

"Sometimes I do my best thinking with them open," he whispered, not allowing his gaze to waver.

Color appeared in her face, and her fingers slowly slid downward, but his own hands reached up and held them in place. And although she could not see his hidden laughter, she was growing ill at ease over his penetrating eyes that she could not escape. Yet, it seemed that her courage grew in the midst of the emotional adversity caused by the man that was so close to her.

"Are you going to take me to your island or not?"

"I'm in a little boat on the trout lake," he began.

"Is it sunny or overcast?"

"Sunny."

"Is the sun at your back?"

"I guess so." He paused for a moment. "Yes. Yes, it is."

She whispered, "Feel the warmth of the sun as it goes through your shirt and relaxes your skin. Can you feel it?"

He found himself slightly nodding at the memory. "There are little gushes of wind blowing across the lake," he remembered out loud.

"How does it feel on your face?"

"Good."

"Peaceful?"

"Peaceful."

"Bring me to your favorite place on the lake," she intoned.

"There is a large boulder at the far end of the lake."

"Do you sit in the boat just looking at this big rock?"

"No. We—I mean I—climb onto the boulder and eat lunch and have a beer."

"What is this big rock like?"

"Big."

"No," she said low but firmly. "Look around the rock. What do you *see*?"

James found himself closing his eyes, and upon the large boulder on which he sat was a thick layer of moss that covered almost the entire top of the rock.

This much he told her.

And growing in the moss were tiny white wildflowers that never meant much to him. A gentle breeze swept passed him that blew up small whitecaps in the dark green water below.

This much he told her.

An eagle gracefully soared above him and a blue heron flew from one tree to another. All around him pine trees born from boulder shores climbed the steep hillside to reach the brilliant, clear blue sky. And behind him, through the woods and into the forest, he could almost feel the deer, beaver, squirrels, and other creatures watching him.

This much he told her.

Upon opening his eyes, he stared at the simple young woman and was filled with awe.

Not once, during the countless visits to the island had he paid attention to the small details about him. He may have touched his surroundings, but he did not really *see* them. He knew that the wind had pushed against his back and pressed upon his face, but she had brought forth a part of his soul that surely did not exist before today.

He was sure that she knew this too, for quiet tears flowed from her. He slowly removed his hands so she could wipe her eyes, but she did not. Almost regrettably, Anna let go of him.

She placed her hands in her lap where her eyes followed and her tears fell. Still she did not wipe her eyes. It came to him that perhaps, if this strange young woman chose to dry her face, she would wipe away the description of the place she wanted to see, but probably never would.

James watched her slowly get up from the bale of hay. He watched her pick up the violin case and turn away from him. She stood there with her chin raised, and pushing her shoulders back, she carried herself across the barn floor to the dark exit. Anna momentarily paused at the threshold and looked back. And upon her face James thought he saw a contented smile, but he wasn't entirely sure in the poorly filtered light. She turned towards the dark passageway and was gone, leaving him alone in the barn.

It was very rare for him to feel alone. This much he knew.

But as he sat there, sitting very still as if any movement might wash away the memory and feeling of what had just taken place, he found himself feeling *very* alone.

This he could not tell her.

His shoulders and spine involuntarily shook which he blamed on the cool, damp, lonely barn. And as he rose to leave, he glanced up to where the barn birds made their home.

Not one swallow bothered to say goodbye.

## CHAPTER 5—THE PEACE TREATY

The sound came from somewhere outside his head. His body automatically swung upright before alertness was allowed to enter. The bedroom was coal black and suddenly coldness hit his bare arms. There—there it was again, and again, and again. James tried to pull his senses together as his feet instinctively made their way out of his bedroom and down the hall. He paused in the living room. Clumsy fingers found the source of light under a lampshade as the knocking continued and persisted like a toothache.

"I'm coming," he growled. "Hold on, I'm coming!"

Turning on the porch light and pushing back the thin curtains that covered the thin window, the visitor was revealed. James stood there, still rocking in the realm of sleep with the cold air pushing against his body. He shut his eyes hard and shook his head in disbelief. The figure, which could have belonged to Anna McManus, stood wrapped in a coat and scarf, hands hidden inside pockets.

"What are you doing here?" he demanded.

"Let me in."

James unlocked the door and she quickly entered the room. Anna shook her upper body as if to rid herself of the outdoor elements. She began to remove her gloves and her coat. Looking about for a moment, she decided to drape the articles over the arm of the big sofa. James remained standing at the open door.

Anna began pulling on one end of her scarf when she abruptly stopped, looked up at him and remarked, "Those things do close, you know."

The scarf joined the other articles on the sofa, and no sooner was the door shut than he asked her again, "What are you doing here?"

"We need to talk."

"We *do*?"

"We do."

"Listen. Where I come from, it's not polite to get a man out of a bed in the middle of the night and expect him to carry on some sort of conversation, which I presume you had planned on doing."

She grinned. "And we are."

He rolled his eyes. "Fine, but at an hour that's more reasonable. This is *not* a reasonable hour! I'm sorry, but this is going to have to wait until later."

James put his hand back on the doorknob and hoped such an indication would prompt his visitor to vacate the premises. But there she stubbornly stood, slowly shaking her head.

"No, Mr. Edwards. This is *not* going to wait 'til later. Although it is usually not my nature to seek out men such as you, I find that our crossing of paths has disturbed our lives. And since it appears that you are staying for a while, I think it would benefit us both if were to come to some understanding of each other."

The woman known as Anna McManus stood before him, so sure of herself, steady and firm in her belief of how life *should* be conducted. He still eyed her in partial dislike, for he had never came upon her type before. James Edwards also harbored a dislike for the woman who brought him into the world. She also had strength but used hers to dominate her husband and son. On the other hand, Anna displayed an inner strength that was entirely different from his mother's. He had been forming an opinion about Anna since their few encounters, and even he himself felt that she possessed a quality of mind that stressed firmness and purpose. James had never met a woman who was so full of spirit, temper, stubbornness, and persistence. He sank into the overstuffed chair and gestured for her to do the same, wrapping his arms around his shivering body.

She looked at him closely. "You look cold."

"Yes, I suppose I am. Where I come from, it's customary to turn the heat down at night."

"Why don't you get yourself dressed in something warmer?" she suggested.

"I'm fine," he lied.

"Your goosebumps do not agree with you."

James looked down at his arms and tried to focus his tired eyes on them.

"Oh, go on," she coaxed with a hint of softness in her voice. "The chill in the air is making you cranky. You get dressed and I'll make some coffee. You never know how long this might take."

He watched her rise from the couch, walk into the kitchen, and turn on a light. His heavy eyes closed, and the rest of his body wanted to curl up in the chair and pretend that this bad dream was just that—a bad dream. But the chill in the air could not be ignored, nor could his unwelcome visitor.

While he put on a clean pair of socks and took cold jeans and a sweatshirt out of the dresser, he could hear the opening of cupboards, water turning on, and something being put together which clanked. She hadn't asked where anything was; he had to give her credit for that. It must be a "woman" thing, he concluded, for one woman to know where another woman puts things.

He stood in the doorway that separated the kitchen from the front room and still wondered if all of this was some sort of fuzzy dream. The young woman at the turquoise-colored stove had a little smile on her face as she wiggled the coffee pot in the center of the red-orange coils. As the water pushed itself up into the glass dome, it made a *blub, blub* noise. The smile on her face grew.

"I'm glad your relatives still have one of these."

"I suppose your folks have one too?" he asked, mocking her mildly.

"Yes, we do. It makes the best coffee I've ever had." She shrugged. "But that's my own opinion."

"Of course it is. And only yours."

The words came out more harshly than he had intended. He thought of apologizing, but thought better of it as he saw that she did not lower her eyes or turn to give him a cold stare.

"Aren't those things horribly slow?" he asked.

"To some people, I suppose they are."

"Jeez, I mean, back in Seattle you could grab an espresso on practically any corner before you could put that contraption together."

Anna adjusted the coffee pot on the coils and the percolating of the liquid picked up speed. She turned a little to face him but kept her eyes on the glass dome that was filled with brown liquid. She casually crossed her arms, then one foot over the other.

She observed, "Yes, it's true, this 'contraption' as you call it does take time. But it also makes people slow down, makes them wait, and that forgotten virtue called patience is discovered or rekindled." Anna looked up at James. "Folks are in too much of a hurry, Mr. Edwards. They forget how to make time for the little and important things in life. Take time to walk along life's paths more often and discover what's there. She paused, then spoke intensively. "Life should not be hurried."

She left him to ponder that thought while she returned her attention to the light blue, round-cornered stove. The small bar of fluorescent light perched under a little hood lit up the stove area and softly glowed around Anna and beyond. The light did not reach James while he leaned against the doorjamb, and unlike other lights, this type was not inviting, so he kept his arms crossed and squinted at the woman who dutifully stood at the stove.

He probably could have heard the humming of batteries in the clock if the coffee pot had not been making the *blub, blub,* noises. But as it did, the wonderful aroma had slowly been filling up the partially lit room. His mind, which was leaning against the door for support, welcomed the richness of the ground beans being drawn out by the boiling water. It created a soothing, almost hypnotic sound that echoed in his head over and over again. His body was totally relaxed, as if it had been taken over by the rich aroma itself.

His eyes fixed themselves upon the woman at the stove and saw that her face was untouched by makeup, as it would be at such an ungodly hour. But obviously it didn't matter to her if she was seen that way. Her hair was brushed for the visit but stuck out in places. His eyes lowered themselves to her sweater and saw that certain curves were there where God intended them to be. Lowing his eyes, he saw more curves rounding out her jeans.

Although his eyes rested upon her, they were still heavy and tired. Basking in the odd light the bulb emitted, he heard Anna drink in the kitchen air.

"Are you done?"

It took a few moments for his hearing to filter and digest her question, which he noticed *wasn't* a question when the door of realization creaked open. Perhaps he didn't mean to do what he did since he still wasn't fully awake and couldn't be accused of the crime. But nonetheless, he was caught in her eyes and decided to sit down at the small table and claim his chair in the outskirts of the strange light. Settling deep into the plain wooden chair, he folded his arms in front and eased into a comfortable position with his legs far in front of him. For the most part he was in semi-darkness, and his mind detected this. In his weakness his eyes felt heavy once again and the square of black glass lulled him into of light sleep. The room spoke in hushed voices. His head bowed forward and his eyelids closed.

Far away a soft voice was humming, and although the cupboards were opening and closing and cups were placed on saucers, his mind was not obligated to respond. And so a warm blanket of mental fog covered him and he heard no more. But then something drew him back. His sense of feeling awoke. She was standing at his side facing him with a hand on his left shoulder.

"It is time," she clearly announced.

He lifted his half-open eyes to hers and noticed a soft smile and warm eyes. Anna removed her hand from his shoulder and took up the other seat, resting her arms on the table. James slid his chair up to the table but anchored an elbow on the surface and supported his chin on a row of knuckles. As he squinted at the woman across from him, the two silently regarded each other as do two animals of the same species, but total strangers to each other.

A silent chuckle ran through James and he repeated her words. "Yes, it is time. It is time for you to say what you have come here to say. Then you will leave, I will go back to sleep, everyone will be happy, and hopefully I won't have huge circles under my eyes tomorrow morning. Tomorrow is *Sunday*, you know. If I should look awful, I will have you to blame. If anyone should ask why I'm so tired looking, I suppose I'll have to think of a creative but honest explanation."

"I suppose. . .but you won't."

"You don't think so?"

Anna shook her head.

"And why not?"

"For starters, who is going to believe you when you try to tell them that I paid you an early morning visit?"

"I would imagine lots of folks, since they probably know you as the peculiar one."

"I've known my neighbors a lot longer than you have Mr. Edwards, and in all the years that I've been growing up with their children, not one person has ever called me peculiar, until now. Have you ever stopped to think that as an outsider, that maybe *you* are the strange one among us?"

James dismissed her words and stared at Anna in a perplexed way.

"So, just what was it that brought you here? I seem to have forgotten. Something about 'understanding each other?' "

"That is correct."

James shifted in his chair.

"Out of sheer curiosity, can you tell me why that would be so damn important to me?"

Anna pulled her chair in and leaned into the table, folding her arms on the table edge and under her chest. Her eyes were on his, and they had no intention of moving elsewhere.

"Before you came here Mr. Edwards, things were just fine. Your uncle was pastor of our little church for just about as many years as I am old. I can understand the need for him and his wife to retire and live in Ireland for a few years. But what I don't understand is why he picked you to replace him."

James stared at her. "Don't you think I'm qualified?"

"I couldn't say. But what I've seen so far, you do have one area mastered."

"And what is that?"

"Your ability to talk about yourself."

"If you would have stayed in church that one Sunday, you would have heard a regular church service after I introduced myself to everyone."

"Oh, I suppose a few old men who can't hear nodded anyway, while the young girls acted stupid and the old ladies had twinkles in their eyes, and the young men felt like they had a rival on their hands."

James moved his chair in and leaned into the table, folding his arms on the table edge and under his chest. His eyes were on hers and they had no intention of moving elsewhere.

"You don't like me, do you?"

His question hung in the silent room, and when it became very uncomfortable, Anna's words were spat at him.

"You don't belong here."

He was frozen by the cruelty of her words. Once again, Anna managed to assault and attack him. His arms slid from the table and his hands dropped to his lap. His eyes could only stare blankly at his lap where his hands lay still. He could not believe what he heard. No one in his entire life had ever told him that he didn't belong.

James wanted to look at the woman across from him and let her see the dismay and hurt on his face. He lifted his eyes and chin and pulled his eyebrows together. He planted his elbows back on the table.

"What makes you think that I don't belong?"

"You are a city boy. A born-and-bred city boy. People like you don't leave the big city of Seattle and plunk yourself in the middle of nowhere for no reason. Least of all to take your uncle's position as pastor of a little church in the middle of a wheat field. Not unless you're running away from something—or someone."

Anna glared at James and his eyes quickly dropped to the table.

"I've answered your question Mr. Edwards. If you want to talk, I'll listen. And just because the rest of the world likes you, don't expect me to. Whatever you want to say to me let it be honest, but just don't take me for stupid."

He focused his eyes on the grain of the table while her words were repeated in his mind. "To talk, to listen, to be honest. But just don't take me for stupid. . ." The young woman across from him was still a stranger, more or less. Did she really need to know why he left Seattle, or should he just tell her that it was none of her damn business? If he did tell her, what was to keep her from telling every living soul around? He would be the laughing stock of Dusty and Colfax, and he was sure that Anna McManus would be laughing the hardest. He could almost feel her pleasure from his embarrassment.

Although he should have initiated the conversation, he found himself noncommittal regarding his own judgment. His courage was reduced to observing the rising steam from his cup. The table that they sat at was not a large table. Perhaps it was the size that bothered

James for it couldn't have been more than four feet wide. Arms and elbows, cups and saucers took up most of the distance, he noted. He also noticed that he was losing his tongue over the quiet, waiting look that Anna McManus trained on him. Seconds ticked by, which turned into minutes. He knew that if the morning hour had been in his favor, he wouldn't be gliding a finger along the wet and warm rim of his coffee cup or toying with the handle.

Anna took her cup between both hands and slowly sipped, not moving the cup too far from her mouth. He brought his cup close to his own but the steam was too hot. There was no pretending in drinking coffee; either you do or you don't. Moments of discomfort could have been disguised between sips here and there. Unfortunately, he was not given that opportunity and had to put his cup down. A heavy sigh followed.

"You're not making this easy on me."

After the words left his mouth, he knew it was the wrong thing to say and cast a look of defeat in her direction. But much to his surprise, she sat there with her content little grin, slowly taking in whatever she saw around her. Anna cocked her head and closed her eyes and asked, "What do you hear, Mr. Edwards?"

"The stupid clock on the wall. Yes, I do hear the clock humming and I've heard it humming one too many times. Who couldn't hear it? This place is *too* quiet. Too *damn* quiet. I don't see how you people can stand it. No fire engines or ambulances blaring, no city traffic that let you feel as if you're one with the human race. And there's no latte stands either."

"So you haven't made peace with your new found solitude?"

"Oh, is that what you call this?" he huffed in annoyance. "Well, I don't see how you can stand it."

"First of all, it's not always constant, unless you want it to be. Second, I take from solitude only what I need from it. You mistake me for a hermit who takes refuge in the vast fields around us. I am not like you, Mr. Edwards, but perhaps, in time, you will learn to live with it, and maybe even come to *appreciate* it. And then, even before you can acknowledge it, you depend upon it daily. You grab bits and pieces of it as if it were a jewel."

She took a slow sip of her coffee and fixed her steady eyes upon his, and in between the next sip she finally said to him, "When you are content with solitude, Mr. Edwards, you will be at peace with yourself."

Silence is a strange thing. It has been cursed and it has been blessed. It cannot be weighed, nor held in the palm of one's hand. But such a simple thing as a clock on a kitchen wall can measure the contemplation of words in a man's mind.

James Edwards squinted at the round-rimmed copper clock and saw that the black arms almost shook hands with the twelve and the two. He swung his narrowing hard eyes back at Anna. The cup in front of him was not embraced by his hands, but rejected as it was pushed across the table. His fingertips on one hand tapped in a four-gaited rhythm against the tabletop while the other hand dug into his cheek, shoving the unshaven flesh upward. The smallest fingertip entered his mouth and was kept motionless in the grip of his teeth. His other hand was picking up speed as well as volume in the dusk of the kitchen. The tapping had turned to thumping and James Edwards' eyes took a turn for the worse, but the woman who sat across from him seemed totally unaffected and continued to sip her coffee while calmly observing her tablemate.

At that moment he found himself pushing his chair away from the table and turning the fluorescent light off. He hurried into the living room, snuffed out the light, and with the help of his hands he made his way through the black room, down the hallway and back to his bedroom.

He did not shut the door quietly, nor did he gently sit himself upon his bed. The man, the pastor, the proud and confused human paced around the room with his arms tightly held against his body. James finally stopped, threw his head back and growled under his breath, "What have I done? What have I done?"

He shut his eyes and the image of another woman smiled sweetly at him. His memory of her was still too fresh to erase her perfumed skin, the feel of her hair in his hands, the sound of her voice, and the laugh that followed after he announced a major life decision. As the woman's voice continued to laugh over and over again, his heart tightened with anger and the wounds of deceit were reopened.

In the other room was another woman who occupied the dark morning hour. She had come to him, to hear him, and she wasn't laughing at him. Yet, the woman whom he left in the dark was different; odd, peculiar, and stirred up parts of his soul that he never knew existed. Anna could not be a threat in any way romantically or physically, for she was a plain, simple individual who lived her life content with serving others at her father's café, and probably would do so for the remainder of her life. Furthermore, he would not have to be convinced that her circle of friends probably went no further than the threshold of the little café.

What did she know about life and its troubles? How could she understand anything of his difficulties while living under the sheltered blanket of wheat fields? He doubted if a man had ever kissed her—but, if he had, it probably was on a dare. No, Anna McManus could not hurt him. James sank on the bed after coming to this conclusion, bowed his head and half-heartedly apologized to God for the anger that had filled him. He did not like such anger to possess him, and he knew it was wrong. But he *was* only human.

Although Anna was not directly the cause of his anger, her fault did lie in the mentioning of quiet time— time to spend licking wounds while they healed. Anna's idea of solitude was fine for her, but his mind was deprived of the background noise of the city when his body wasn't on the move. He missed the sounds that came from the inner city: taxis honking, buses screeching up and down steep grades, and ferryboats blasting their departure horns. And the people. He greatly missed the diverse blend of cultures that gave Seattle its unique flavor as a city. James Edwards sat on the bed and breathed deeply. His heart ached for Seattle at 2:23 a.m.

He reached over and turned on the bedside lamp and knew he had to go out and say *something* in defense of his behavior. While 2:24 turned into 2:30, he wondered if Anna had gotten back in to her outdoor clothes and quietly slipped out. But he hadn't heard so much as a creak in the house, so he continued to sit and wonder. Could it be possible that she was still sitting in the dark? What person would stay in a cold, black kitchen in the early morning hours, unless *she* fell asleep, waiting?

As he sat wondering, he heard footsteps within the house. They paused, and then he heard a familiar click in the hallway, more footsteps, a pause, and then the footsteps faded. James waited for the sound of the front door to open and close, but it did not come.

The thought of Anna's wrath waiting for him did not help his body rise off the mattress. If it was anything close to that morning in the barn, he felt a lot safer behind his door. Eventually, he ventured out into the hallway that was dark except for the bedside lamplight that strayed from the room. A few steps farther on, he caught sight of the reason for the familiar clicking he had heard. It took only a moment or two for his facial muscles to relax and his mouth to curl upward. The owner of the footsteps within the house had turned the heater to seventy degrees.

The living room was not as dark as it should have been. Untouched articles of clothing were revealed on the couch's arm by a strange light that glowed dimly within the kitchen. Larger-than-life shadows seemed to sprawl against the walls, loom in corners, and hang on the ceiling. Shadows were pulled away from behind their secret homes like taffy.

The former city dweller observed this strange light

from the kitchen doorway. On the table sat a shapely object of clear glass from which emerged a tongue of flame. The young woman at the table was now resting her head on her arms and her eyes appeared closed. After a long period of hesitation, James cautiously crossed the kitchen floor to further observe his guest. The soft light gave her features a younger, warmer appearance, and even the shadows under her eyelashes danced on her lightly freckled face. His glances shared time between being mesmerized by the new object, and by the sleeping woman who bathed in the yellow light.

In a way he felt strange peering down on her, as if he were violating some personal right, but she was unaware of his doings. He was struck by the thought that this woman, as peculiar as he had ever known a woman to be, had something within her that he *needed* his existence in such a bleak land. What it was he did not exactly know, for it was more of a tugging of instinct that told him not to ignore or shut this woman out of his life. She had to be included in it, woven into it, and whether or not they would have anything in common to act as the yarn did not matter.

He was sure that this woman of humble background could fill in the hours when the silence around him cultivated unwelcome memories of another Eve.

James sat down and carefully brought his chair closer to the table. Perhaps the soft yellow light which touched her hair was an invitation for James to do also. Perhaps he was thinking of the morning in the barn when she held his face in her hands. Was it the oddity of the situation that was beginning to appeal to him? His mouth twitched under his own questioning. But a hand was already hovering near her head until it touched her hair. What would she think, James wondered, if suddenly her sleep were disturbed and upon awakening she caught him stroking her head?

As this thought chuckled through his brain the heel of his hand grazed her cheek, causing Anna to stir. His fingers quickly retreated, and in a moment of genius reaction they grabbed for the coffee cup. By the time she breathed deeply and lifted her head off her arms while beginning to focus her eyes, James was sitting calm and relaxed while sipping his cold coffee. His mouth cringed from the cold and bitterness of it, and for a moment it stayed on his taste buds until it was forced down. Anna sat up, looking dazed, and folded her arms in her lap. James reached for the cups and, going over to the sink, poured the coffee down the drain. He refilled the cups with fresh, hot coffee and brought them back to the table where Anna was in the process of covering a yawn.

She reached for the cup with both hands and slid it closer to her. With her eyes still fixed on the tabletop, James took this opportunity to begin.

"I owe you an apology, Miss McManus. I lost my temper. . . and. . . well, I. . ."

Anna gave each word a deserved tone and distance. "You left me in the dark."

"Yes, I did," he admitted. "Do I have your forgiveness?"

His own ears knew that he spoke with perhaps the most sincerity he had ever asked of one person. He had asked it right from his heart and a hand was placed over it to further declare his intentions. But the woman across from him did not make haste to answer.

Anna raised her cup and studied the rising steam. She inhaled deeply and kept her eyes on the steady wave.

"Would your conscience have a better day if I did forgive you?"

"Yes, it would," he admitted.

"Hmm. . ." Anna got up and strolled the length of the floor. She took sips of her coffee while studying the shadows on the walls. "Hmm," she mouthed again.

"I was thinking that maybe the ceiling lights would be too much, so I turned on the fluorescent light at the stove. Apparently that sort of light does not agree with you."

She leaned her backside against the counter and crossed her legs.

"As I sat here in the dark which you had kindly provided, I tried to sift out several possibilities for a reason for you to react the way you did. And while I was doing so, I thought of my soft pillow on my nice bed in my room upstairs."

"But you stayed."

"I could have left, and as I said, for a brief moment I let the idea in my head. But that would have been too easy."

Anna paused and tapped an index finger against her lips, then a finger slowly lowered itself and was gentle in its reprimand.

"I whispered out loud, 'You're going to have to do worse than that, Mr. Edwards.' I discovered that oil lamp in your aunt's pantry. They come in handy during the winter when we have power outages, or when lights go *out*."

Over the rim of the coffee cup her eyes shifted straight in his direction. James folded his arms and pulled his shoulders inward and crossed his legs. While he suffered under her stare, he gently nibbled at the inner flesh of his mouth; and in the silence he waited.

"Now, Mr. Edwards, I know the time you spent in your room was not entirely pleasant. But it gave you plenty of time to think things over. Talking never hurts, you know. When we don't, that makes things harder to bear. I am here to listen, or you can tell me to get my coat and leave." Anna paused. "Which will it be?"

James took a lung full of air from the room and then gave it back. He hung his head, gestured for Anna to have a seat, and then cleared his throat.

He whispered, "Have you ever been told by someone that they don't want anything to do with you if you become a pastor?"

Anna was listening.

"You've known someone for years, fallen in love, gone through the process of becoming a pastor, and then ask that person to spend the rest of their life with you, and—" He paused, but continued with hardness grabbing at his voice. "She *laughed* at the idea of being a pastor's wife. She laughed so hard I thought she would break a rib."

James had to look at the black window. His throat was tightening from anger, humiliation, and the shame of his emotions being on display. He tried to clear his throat but could not, and he was sure that the woman who sat across from him would think him less of a man. James lowered his face and covered it with a hand, but then he felt another gentle hand cover his. This gesture took him by such surprise that he unveiled his face and looked up. She reached out with her other hand, turned it palm side up, and laid it on the table. He took up her hand and, pulling both of them together, gave them more than a gentle squeeze. There were words that wanted to run out of him, but the tightness in his throat squeezed them back.

In the semi-darkness that mingled with the soft glow of yellow light, the kitchen was warm and still. Neither of them spoke. Perhaps it was the combination of elements in the room that made him take note of the stillness. Perhaps it was Anna's warm hands upon his that made him feel safe. During this period of mutual silence, he didn't feel as if he had to fill the void. This was new to him, for no other female which he knew was so different. Letting his eyes rise from their joined hands to her face, he studied her until he found his tongue.

"I appreciate you turning the heater on, and for bringing out this lamp. You'll have to tell me more about your power outages sometime."

"Maybe. . ."

If he was going to ask, he had to do it now.

"Anna—I need your help."

She cocked her head to one side. "What kind of help?"

"I was thinking, that since you probably know everyone in church, you might accompany me on some of my visits. You know, to give me some sort of background on the families so I—"

James felt her hands slipping off his, and she brought them back to her body, crossing them under her chest and slowly shook her head.

"I'm sorry, but I won't be able to do that."

"Why not?" James asked.

"*That* is something which you must do on your own. You will come to know them quickly and gain their confidence in no time. Besides, it's *you* they want to see. Not me."

"It would be a lot easier if you were with me."

"It would," she agreed.

"Can't blame a guy for trying," he acknowledged, smiling. Then he added, "One more thing."

"One more thing?" Anna raised her eyebrows. "Depends what the *thing* is."

"Well," he drew the word out on his breath, "I was wondering, if you could spend a little time with me each week. We could just talk. Or, if you didn't want to talk, we could watch TV or something. *Anything*, would be better than being out here alone." He looked at her hopefully.

Anna was silent and slowly straightened her spine. Her crossed arms did not move from their perch. James had seen Anna McManus fewer times than he could count on one hand, but he knew that her changing posture might not be in his favor. He lowered his voice, and speaking slowly and cautiously, he leaned into the table in the hope that Anna would perceive the extent of his sincerity. His heart *felt* sincere and his mind *told* him that he was sincere; and that was enough for James to venture forward.

"If you could just be here with me. I could do the talking if you didn't feel like talking. And I won't talk if you don't feel like listening. Just be here with me."

He found his words tripping over each other in his effort to make her understand.

Anna did not speak right away. Her eyes wanted their turn in mocking him. His hope in her suddenly became a cause for ridicule.

"So, the whole point is that you need me to be your survival kit, or something like that."

James started to open his mouth but could only mutter, "But I'll . . ." when Anna pushed herself away from the table and walked some distance away from him.

"She *really* must have made an impact on you, for you to be begging for *my* companionship. Why me? Am I not a threat to you?"

Anna rolled her eyes toward the ceiling and shook her head. "Oh, stupid, ignorant me! How could I be? Of course I'm not! How could I be? Any fiancée of yours *must* have been as much, if not more handsome than yourself. That is how things are. Aren't they? Good-looking guys *cringe* at the thought of being alone with a plain, ordinary female. Unless—unless they are *very* desperate. Unless. . .they feel that their sanity is in danger of being lost. It is then that they will tolerate women like me." She paused. "We are wanted only for our presence."

The kitchen was silent, and the clock's humming could be heard.

"If you are looking for a survival kit," she chewed the cold words up as she spoke, "they sell those in stores!"

Rising from her chair, she looked at the floor for a moment, then back up at him.

"Well, all things considered, you can rest assured that I will *never* bother you again. Goodbye."

She made her way to the front room and put on her coat and scarf. James stood on the threshold of the kitchen and watched her. He watched her button each button with her head bent, and then in the dimly lit room he watched her shoulders begin to shake. He found himself crossing the room and turning on a small light that was close to the upright piano. Turning around slowly to face her, he sat down on the piano bench.

The young woman in front of him was crying, and as she put her gloves on she managed to say, "No, Mr. Edwards, you may not use me. I have had my share of that pie. If this place doesn't occupy your mind enough, go back to Seattle. If you want someone to fill in the empty hours so you won't be constantly reminded of her, adopt a pet. Get a hobby. You pass by women like me every day without giving them a second glance or a second thought. I have often wondered what men like you would want from a woman like myself. Thanks to you, *now* I know."

She wiped a hand under her nose and James started to rise from the piano bench.

"Anna, I'm sorry. . ."

"Don't!" she hissed. She quickly backed away and went to the door. "At least I have *one* friend who I can count on. It's pathetic, don't you think, that a piece of wood is worth more to me than human friendship? My violin, Mr. Edwards, has never hurt me or has ever asked for anything in return. It . . .only gives. Men. . .only take."

Anna's gloved hand quickly opened the door, and

in her wake the thin glass rattled in its frame.

The few seconds of panic that followed did not cause hesitation in his mind. God had given James a wonderful memory and an ear for music. His mind flashed back to the barn and the music immediately filled his head. Swiveling on the bench to face the keys, he awoke them abruptly from their slumber. His fingers were a blur on the keys as he pushed down harder and harder, crying out loud for the music to bring her back.

And upon the back of his neck he felt cool air brush by, and felt her presence behind him. His trembling fingers hung just above the keys, his eyes pressed shut. When he opened them he found her facing him, standing next to the piano with tears running down her face—and her expression was one James would never forget.

A breath of astonishment escaped from her. "You play the. . .?"

Her eyes were wide as they looked over the keys, then at him, then at the keys again.

"You—you played the song that I was playing in the barn. But, how'd you know—?"

"Was it okay?" James asked softly.

Anna smiled. "You played as if you had listened inside my head. You played a dream of mine, a dream that I've been waiting for years for someone to play it on the piano."

James remembered, "That morning in church—you had your friend with you in your head. What were you playing?"

"I can't remember."

"Think! Think!" he implored her.

"I can't!"

"Try humming it!"

She was shaking her head. "I can't, not without my violin!"

There was a long pause.

"Anna McManus, I *need* you—like you *need* your violin."

The silence in that early morning hour would be hard to describe, and the time that followed would be hard to measure, for there are some things in life which are too precious for words.

James reached out his right hand to her. "I need you to be my friend." He said simply, then paused. "Nothing less, nothing more. . ."

Anna's lips echoed, "Nothing less, nothing more. . ."

The young pastor and the young woman eyed each other.

"This handshake will be our—our peace treaty," James declared.

Anna removed a glove and placed her hand in his. It was warm and stronger than he had expected or imagined—and James was reluctant to let it go.

At the door that he held open for her, she turned to him and said, "By the way, if you want me to stay awake and not create music in my head in seven hours, your sermon better be a damn good one."

With that, she was gone.

And while the rest of the world slept, James poured himself another cup of coffee and rewrote his sermon.

And, in the third row on the right side of the little church sat Miss Anna McManus, surrounded by her happy and relieved family.

## CHAPTER 6—THE SONG OF WINE

The duties of pastor of his little church kept him busier than he ever imagined. April went by in a blur. May seemed to disappear in a blink. June appeared full with events and appointments which filled up the calendar that hung beside the telephone. There were people who needed to be visited: people who needed counseling, the temporarily sick, and those for whom eventually he would say the final prayers as the last page came to a close in their book of Life.

James visited the wives and the husbands. He tried to get a feel for what was important in their lives. Little by little he began to feel like he belonged. People greeted him on the street and waved as they passed on the road. He walked with farmers on their land that they were proud of, and wives offered plates of cookies and cups of coffee on his visits.

His eyes moved from the calendar to the clock that hung above the phone. It read 8:58 p.m. James glanced at his watch. It also read 8:58 p.m.

Opening the refrigerator door, he reached inside and felt the cool bottle of blush wine. Next to it were a few cans of beer for himself. It was the third or fourth time since supper that he checked the bottle. He was thinking of popping the wine in the freezer for a few minutes when her knock sounded on the front door.

Outside, they sat on the steps and listened to the night.

Once in a while, a Killdeer bird flew out from a nearby pasture singing its haunting call, "Killdeer. . .killdeer. . .killdeer," until the sound faded down the fields and into the darkness.

"Pretty," Anna whispered, "I always did like them."

It was nice, he told himself, to be able to just enjoy a woman's company without worrying whether he was saying too much or too little. Anna was comfortable and he liked that. It made his soul peaceful when he was with her. It was hard to describe what he felt, other than his insides grew warm and fuzzy. Of course, it could have been a combination of blissful contentment mixed with two beers that gave him courage to ask, "Miss Anna, what excites you?"

She laughed, almost gagging on a swallow of wine. "What? Oh gosh, let's see. . ." Her tongue clucked a few times as she pondered his question, then held out her glass. "Pour me some more and let me think a sec."

James picked up the nearly empty bottle that sat between them, poured the remaining contents out, and slowly, almost regretfully, put the bottle back on the steps.

Her eyes were closed, but her lightly freckled face

revealed a mind that was searching, a mind that was opening windows and doors. He no longer wanted to stand on the outside looking in. James wanted the key to those doors, but he also knew he had to be patient.

He held onto his beer quietly so the can wouldn't make a sound.

He watched her take a sip of the wine that must have been warm on her tongue. He watched her breasts rise and fall as she took a deep breath and slowly let it out.

On the sweet June evening breeze, her voice blew gently against his ears.

"New fallen snow that glistens and hasn't been touched by a human being. Tulips, daffodils, and crocuses blooming after the bleakness of winter. Rushing wind through a tree, or between windowpanes opened just so. The humming and buzzing of voices and warmth at Christmas concerts. The warmth of fireplaces, crackling of sparks, the glow of kerosene lamps. Power outages that last for days. The intoxicating aroma of a freshly cut pumpkin.

She smiled and continued, "Listening to Nat King Cole, Glenn Miller, and George Winston solo on piano. Going to the barn on stormy days and listening to rain pounding on the roof. It is beautiful when it echoes within the old walls. Other times it accompanies my violin. It is then that I find Mom and Dad cuddled up in a blanket, thermos and coffee cups in tow, sitting quietly against the bales below, watching the steam rise from the cups and listening, just listening. . ."

She drank what was left in her glass, stared at it, and narrowed her eyes. Setting the glass down, she placed a hand on his thigh and whispered, "Well, goodnight," and pushed off, her feet carrying her away from the porch, away from him, fading into the darkness.

With that she was gone. He would have said something if his tongue had been in working order, which at that moment, it was not. Whatever would have come forth would have been out of place, and regretted. He was grateful that muteness overcame him—this once.

As the sound of her footsteps faded down the dirt driveway, his ears strained to pick up the slightest sound.

And then, he heard nothing.

The night was too quiet when he heard his own breathing; as slight as it was.

The night felt cooler, blacker, and emptier.

With both hands wrapped around the beer can, he crushed it; the requester of the song.

From the hollows of his soul he groaned, "Oh, God!"

He sat on the porch steps a while. Then he left the bottle, the glass, and the cans on the steps as he went inside.

He lay awake in bed for a long, long time.

He wished for next week to hurry and come, and he wished. . .for other things.

## CHAPTER 7—HARVEST MOON

He had parked his truck on the outskirts of the gravel parking lot on purpose. Tonight he wanted to be alone, in his truck, facing the horizon that was changing hues every few minutes. This was his favorite time of the day. From the view of his truck, he recognized quite a few people from his church. Others he thought he had seen in town. The rest who trickled into the Social Hall were total strangers to him.

His job as pastor required visiting people, people sharing their personal troubles over the phone, and an occasional baptism, wedding, or burial. It wasn't that he didn't enjoy being around other people. If that were the case, he would have never considered being a pastor, or vowed to accept the rigors of life that were attached to it. It required so much emotional strength from him that by the end of the week he felt completely drained and needed Anna's visits and quiet evenings to restore a state of balance. He had come to cherish the solitude that dusk usually offered.

The sea of vehicles made their way closer to his as the parking lot filled up. Several folks acknowledged his presence by nodding or waving, and a few wished him a good evening. As they walked towards the hall, James imagined them talking about him having recently taken up smoking a pipe and wondering why he was sitting in his truck alone. Did they not understand that he was one of them? Must a pastor act a certain way just because he was a pastor, and not allow his flock to see that he was human too? He remembered Anna telling him once, "From time to time, people need solitude, a chance to be alone in a place where nothing is asked of us, and the only voice we hear is our own." As one day was ending and another not far away, James couldn't agree more.

Every evening at dusk, while the world put away its work for the day, James Edwards settled down somewhere with his pipe and black-cherry tobacco. Tonight would be no different as he leaned his head against the trucks' head rest. A nice breeze came into the cab and tickled the hair on his arm that rested on the open window. Soon he would have to think about going inside the Hall. Think about tightening up his tie and slipping his jacket over his white dress shirt.

But right now he only paid attention to the sky before him as the end of the day was drawing near. The sun was shaking out her colors before she put them away during the last days of September. Streaks of pink and lavender brushed the sky and James smiled and thanked God for this gift of a sunset. He took a puff on his pipe and glanced in his side view mirror and wondered if Anna had arrived yet; if she was coming at all.

During their last front porch visit, he had asked her if she would be going to the Harvest Dance. She did not give a definite yes or no, but said that if she *did* go, it would *not* be considered a date; *that* she was very clear about. It was explained to him that as soon as one person labels such inquiries, and if the other person does show up, it is then considered a date. Anna detested the word "date," because from what she saw, people seemed to go out of their way to impress the other person, to become someone they were not. He had laughed at her little speech at the time, but knew only too well that she spoke honestly and truthfully for herself, and also for him.

Not once in the past seven months had he brought up the subject of dating. There was no need to. Since the birth of their mutual agreement, in the understanding that their friendship would consist of "nothing less, nothing more," they had been enjoying each other's company to the fullest.

During his weekly visits at the homes of church members, he was surprised how many mothers tried setting him up with their eligible daughters. At first it was somewhat flattering and amusing, but after a while these so called "visits" pertaining to personal or family problems, studying the Bible with him, questioning their faith, wondering how to serve God better in their lives, and complaining about grocery bills turned into discussions surrounding their lovely, charming daughter, or daughters. A few of the more outspoken mothers even had the audacity to mention how happy his uncle was with his aunt while ministering as a couple for more than thirty years in the same church. And although they meant well, he was beginning to hear one too many times, "Every man needs a good woman beside him."

James inhaled deeply and shut his eyes and muttered out loud. "But not all women are willing to stand beside a man after he has decided to become a pastor."

Getting out of the truck with his pipe clenched between his teeth, he removed it and took in one last deep breath of the cooling air about him. James imagined the cleansing air swirl within his lungs, making its way to different parts of his body and finally to his heart. "How precious is the heart when you say it is love, but how easily you toss it away. . ." he thought to himself. James emptied his pipe against a tire, put it back in the cab, smoothed his tie, and put on his jacket.

The sun had gone down by now and the few windows from the Social Hall spilled inviting light onto the parking lot. James kept looking around him for Anna's familiar old truck, but did not see it. The evening would be long and probably miserable if she did not show up. Maybe he could put in his fifteen or twenty minutes and then escape for some fresh air—only he would be heading for his truck, wondering where she was. James could not be too upset with her since she did not promise to come. He climbed the six steps and looked out at the parking lot again, but the blanket of night would not permit his eyes past the first rows of vehicles.

The door opened from behind, spilling more light around him as three men with graying hair and potbellies sucked in fresh air as if they were suffocating. They all greeted him cheerfully.

"Good Evening, Pastor Edwards."

"Glad to see you, Pastor Edwards."

"Hope you enjoy yourself, Pastor Edwards."

James responded pleasantly, "Evening, gentlemen! Tuckered already?"

"Women! Get 'em near a dance floor and they'll want to dance all evening. Oh, my heart is a-beating!" wheezed one man, leaning against the wall.

"Are you going to be all right?" asked James a bit anxiously.

"Ah, don't worry 'bout us," said one.

"When we get tired, we'll have our wives dance with you!" joked another, and then the other two laughed with him.

James grinned and shook his head at the first man, patting his shoulder. "She's your wife, not mine!"

He closed the door behind him leaving the three men laughing on the other side. Right away, music from the live band at the front of the large room filled his ears. The nonparticipant dancers stood at the back of the room with one hand around Styrofoam cups and the other in their jeans pocket. The opposite sex formed small informal huddles where they showed little concern over the choices at hand while plotting and scheming who was going to end up with whom. James was glad that he didn't have to partake in that particular ritual of youth.

Making his way past the teens, he ended up at the

punch table with Mrs. Krumbly serving with another woman. Hanging from the front of the table was a banner that read, "Ladies Auxiliary Club." Around the punch bowl and cups were loads of cookies and other baked goods that could be had for a "donation," according to a small sign taped to the front of a tin coin can.

"Pastor Edwards! What a nice surprise!" beamed Mrs. Krumbly.

"Evening, Mrs. Krumbly."

James wondered if she was surprised to see him all of a sudden, or was she surprised at the thought that he might enjoy an evening of dancing. Was it so hard to imagine him away from the pulpit? Was it so difficult for his flock to understand that he had a life outside of the church?

"Pastor Edwards, I would like you to meet the newest member of our club. This is Mrs. Cynthia Sullivan."

James turned to the older woman and extended both his hands towards one of hers. He gently patted it and smiled. When he was introduced to a younger woman, he smiled and shook hands in a different way. The older generation thought their pastor was charming and kind, just by the way he shook hands with them. He was reminded of this often at the local barbershop where his congregation went for male gossip and an occasional hair trim.

"It's very nice to meet you, Mrs. Sullivan."

She and her husband were fairly new to his church and usually took up a back pew. Mrs. Sullivan smiled a small bashful smile, and quietly replied, "Thank you.

My husband and I enjoy your services."

"Thank you. I'm glad to have you and your husband join us."

Giving her hands a gentle squeeze again, he let go, and pushing back his jacket, stuck his hands in his pockets.

"Are you having a good time?" inquired Mrs. Krumbly.

He shrugged slightly. "Just got here, actually."

James casually eyed the couples dancing, and the folks who rested in chairs that lined the walls. They bent their heads together in deep conversation, cupping a hand to an ear, giving an occasional nod. Laughing. All around him were people, though not one of them was the one who he was waiting for.

"Are you looking for someone, Pastor Edwards?"

James turned back to Mrs. Krumbly, who smiled sweetly up at him.

"Well, kind of."

She leaned forward a bit and with a twinkle in her eyes she whispered, "I was talking to Polly—I mean Mrs. McManus, the night before last." She leaned in for emphasis. "She said the whole family is coming."

"The *whole* family?" James repeated.

"Well, I believe so. . .yes."

James could just see Anna's brothers giving her a hard time the moment they saw her dressed up. He almost wanted to be there to protect her from such sibling silliness. He wanted Anna with him on the dance floor, all night long, just the two of them. He was sensing a deep feeling of protectiveness and greediness that was gradually overcoming him, and as these new feelings took hold of him, he was surprised how strong and demanding they were. James admitted to himself that these feelings were a first towards any female he had ever known. Should they be frightening him? He didn't know, and right now he really didn't care. He could not imagine letting her go into another man's arms, especially not after so many months wondering what it would feel like to *finally* be holding Anna McManus.

"Pastor Edwards? Pastor Edwards?"

James had wandered so far into his thoughts that Mrs. Krumbly felt the need to gently tug on his sleeve. He glanced down at the woman who had a mixture of concern and curiosity on her face.

"Pastor Edwards, are you all right?"

"Never better," he answered cheerfully. "Never better."

"You looked so far away that—oh—is that them? I do believe it is. Good—they're here."

Turning towards the back of the hall he saw the McManus kids wasting no time scattering themselves in search of their friends. Richard McManus emerged through the growing crowd shaking hands with friends and neighbors while Polly was searching the room with her eyes. She turned her head in his direction, and when she caught sight of James, she excused herself from her husband's side and quickly made her way over to the Ladies Auxiliary Club table.

"Good evening, Pastor Edwards." She nodded and smiled at the two women behind the table. "Good to see you, Mrs. Krumbly. Hello, Mrs. Sullivan." The two ladies greeted Anna's mother with more smiles, and asked her to send the family over their table to help support the Ladies Auxiliary Club.

After the necessary greetings, Mrs. McManus said that she needed to steal Pastor Edwards for a moment. James excused himself, promising to come back later for some punch and homemade goodies. When they had moved a short distance away from the table, Mrs. McManus opened her purse and took out something square and dark purple.

"Here, this is for you."

James accepted the velvet article, which had a black twisted braid attached to it. He opened it and found blank lines on faded paper. James softly chuckled and gave Anna's mother a cautious glance.

"Now, this wouldn't be a dance card, would it?"

Mrs. McManus explained, "I was cleaning out a bunch of old stuff the other day when I stumbled upon it. This was my mother's. And yes, it is very old, but I want you to have it. I hope and trust that you will give it to someone whom you care about—someone who will cherish this for a long time."

James caressed the soft velvet, and glancing toward the main door of the hall, he asked, "Do you think she'll come?"

"Well, she was all dressed and looking very nice, I'll admit, but she was sitting on the front porch watching the sunset for the longest time. I just hope that it didn't put her in one of her inspirational moods." Mrs. McManus let out a sigh and could only give a sympathetic shrug with her shoulders. "I don't know what to say. Just keep your chin up, and, it probably wouldn't hurt if you said a handful of prayers."

Excusing herself, she went off in search of her husband.

James stood there with a heavy heart, picturing Anna on her porch taking in the same beautiful sky he was looking at earlier. And oh yes, it *definitely* would have put her in one of her moods. He allowed his chin to fall toward his chest.

The gift from Anna's mother was held tight in his hand. Mrs. McManus was very kind to have made such a gesture. He decided right then, that her expression of love for her daughter would not be wasted. James fumbled inside his jacket pocket and found a pen. He opened up the dance card and wrote down a few things. Now all he had to do was casually slip out for some fresh air and keep on walking to his waiting truck.

He would find her, somewhere, making love to her violin. She would put it down, and he would slip the dance card's soft cord over her hand, and watch it sway as she danced with him.

James quickly put the pen and the dance card inside his jacket, and as he turned to leave, he took a few steps and looked ahead of him. But as he was making his exit, his feet held fast to the floor because his eyes told them to.

~*~

She stood with her arms in front of her, fingers intertwined, watching the others with uncertainty; like a beautiful doe in a meadow, wanting to partake in what it had to offer, yet ever on guard. Eventually she turned her head, and when she saw him, she did not move. He thought he saw her give a sigh of relief, relax her shoulders and smile a little. Cautiously James and Anna walked toward each other and paused.

"Good evening," she whispered.

"It is now," James spoke slowly and sincerely while Anna turned her eyes towards the floor and he saw pink rise in her freckled checks. It had been a long time since he had seen a woman blush. He quickly cleared his throat, and reaching inside his jacket, he produced the dance card. As she stared at it, she covered her mouth with her hand as to hide a smile, but it was too late for he had already seen it. Anna looked at him, then back at the velvet card and slowly touched it.

"Where did you find this?"

"I'm sorry, but I cannot reveal my source. Here, this is for you to keep."

He handed her the card and added, "As you can see Miss Anna, the first and last dances are spoken for. The rest are up to you."

She carefully opened the old dance card, and true to his word, in his handwriting was JAMES EDWARDS written on the first line. Anna held out her left hand and James carefully slipped the soft braid on her wrist.

Offering a hand to her, she put her left hand on his shoulder, and in one smooth motion he pulled her close to him. His arm around her waist was firm, and to his embarrassment, he could feel his heart beat rapidly. Just the same, he felt another heart beat, one that was just as uneasy as his. They began to sway to Nat "King" Cole's *Unforgettable* which did not help ease the sentimental swelling in his chest. It had been years since his thumping heart made him so self-conscious.

And it dawned on him that he was *finally* holding

Anna. Not just in a thought or a dream. She was in the flesh and was holding him. James put his check against hers and relished the feel of her skin, savored the feel and fragrance of her hair, and couldn't believe she was *his*, at least for a while.

The music drew to a close and folks around them either stayed or dispersed to the folding chairs against the walls. They stood for what seemed like eternity, both afraid to look at each other, afraid of revealing unspoken words.

Out of nowhere, a plump, bubbly woman rushed up to them and broke the awkward silence.

"Pastor Edwards, my husband is being such an absolute bore tonight. He wants to park his butt and gab with his buddies instead of dancing with me." She confessed with a giggle, "He said that you look like the type that could shake a leg!"

James looked at her in astonishment. "He said that huh?"

He glanced uneasily at Anna, who grinned back at him and whispered, "I'll be waiting outside."

The plump, giggling woman led James across the dance floor. He tried catching glimpses of Anna, but his perspiring dance partner kept spinning him around. The spot where Anna had stood was empty. His heart sank and he detested his dance partner who knew nothing of the awful crime she had committed.

Thankfully, the song ended but the woman whose name he did not know, nor cared to know, wanted to dance another dance. She stood there close to James, huffing and puffing with beads of sweat rolling down next to her ears. Gathering up as much graciousness as he could muster, Pastor Edwards patted her moist hand, thanked her for the dance and quickly excused himself.

Out on the porch, shadows stretched before them with help from the light of the open door behind them. The words he spoke were private but not hushed, and while in deep conversation, he would not have noticed until too late that a third shadow had slithered into the light. Anna had changed the conversation as smoothly as a hot knife would slice through butter. The shadow began to shorten and withdraw from the light.

Without turning around, Anna exclaimed, "Mrs. Barker, is that you?"

The shadow almost managed to make its escape. James, then Anna, turned around on the steps to face a very embarrassed and perplexed woman, who usually was regarded as the best when it came to keeping her composure under trying circumstances.

James stood up and greeted her with a light handshake.

"Evening, Mrs. Barker."

She inclined her head ever so slightly. "Pastor Edwards."

Mrs. Barker raised her chin and lightly lifted the corners of her mouth and nodded at James. But then her eyes swung down to Anna. They were cold and dark, overflowing with spite. James did not understand what was taking place. He knew Mrs. Barker liked to display herself in a domineering and arrogant way, but this was different. Anna, on the other hand, sat quietly with her hands around her knees, leaning back against the railing, her eyes steady and strong.

In their unspoken battle, Anna was holding her

ground with as much determination as the older woman. Whatever was going on, James was going to put an end to it.

"Was there something you needed, Mrs. Barker?" James asked at last. The intense confrontation between the two women ceased, and Mrs. Barker pulled herself together.

"As a matter of fact, yes. I was looking for you because you had promised to save a dance for my daughter. You haven't forgotten, have you?" she asked, too sweetly.

James paused for a few moments, and he hoped that what he was thinking wasn't showing on his face. It was very clear to him that until he learned more, this woman was someone whom he had to watch closely.

Offering his arm to the older woman, he confessed, "I'm afraid I did. My apologies." As they turned toward the door, James winked at Anna and then abandoned her to the night.

Once inside the stuffy, noisy room, James was paired up to the younger woman who looked much like her mother. The daughter seemed to keep an eye on her mother, who was gloating with pride at the sight of her daughter being held by the young pastor. Only the mother seemed to be enjoying herself, for the daughter did not glance at her dance partner, nor speak to him. It was obvious that she was being forced to do something she detested.

He did feel a little pity for her and offered, "If you don't want to do this, I'll understand."

The young woman finally looked at him, but instead of a sympathetic smile she glared at him. "What

part of *this* don't you understand? Just *look* at her!"
She gestured with a nod of her head toward her mother.

Mrs. Barker was speaking to some women who was
near her and pointing in their direction, making it
known that it was *her* daughter who was dancing with
the eligible pastor. As he was beginning to turn away
from Mrs. Barker, he noticed that her attention was
diverted elsewhere. By the time he had completed the
circle, the mother of his dance partner was gone.

~*~

The rubbing sound of pantyhose being squished by
a pair of legs filled Anna's ears when the door to the
ladies' restroom opened, and a plump figure entered.
Anna stood at the mirror carefully touching up her
lipstick when a voice from behind her sarcastically
sighed, "Do you really think that is going to *help*?"

Anna put the lipstick back in its case and into her
dress pocket, but as she turned to leave, Mrs. Barker
blocked her way. Anna let out a sigh of annoyance and
said, "Get out of my way."

A twisted grin spread over the older woman's face
while she crossed her arms in front of her.

"I am going to say this only once, you miserable
little ass. Leave Pastor Edwards *alone*. He is meant for
*my* daughter. She will make him the *perfect* wife. *You,*
on the other hand, are not fit for *anyone*."

Suddenly the little room was filled with Anna's
insulting laughter.

"Oh yes, they did make a wonderful looking
couple, didn't they? Did you see how your *happy*
daughter was smiling and laughing? Did you notice
how she couldn't keep her eyes off him? Wait! That

wasn't a happy look at all. In fact, I'd say that was the picture of misery. Wouldn't you?"

It had come fast and totally unexpectedly—Anna's face was hit with a fist that sent her reeling backwards, hitting the sink. In the moments that followed, she couldn't stop her hand from reaching for her face to offer it sympathy, and although it was a noble act on her part, it did not lessen the pain. Her cheek stung and felt hot and tears started to fill her eyes, but Anna's rising anger suppressed some of the feeling. Uncoiling within her being, contempt for this excuse of a human filled her eyes, but the older woman did not so much as flinch. "Why you call yourself a Christian is beyond me!" Anna hissed.

"How dare you!" gasped Mrs. Barker.

She almost took a step forward but Anna was quicker.

"No, how dare *you*!" She was standing very close to the woman who would have been her mother-in-law if fate and circumstance had not intervened. After so many years, it felt almost victorious to stare down into the dark eyes of the devil. The blood that ran through her veins was hot and fast. It seemed more like venom than blood.

Anna's voice hardly seemed like her own as she spat, "Now, *you* are going to listen to *me*! I will *not* bear the blame any more for your son's poor judgment that night. What happened was *not* my fault and I have no intention of feeling guilty for something that I wasn't involved in. If *you* can't handle the truth, that's your problem, not mine. Oh, and regarding Pastor Edwards, he is reserved for no one. Only God knows if anyone is."

Mrs. Barker seemed to ponder her words as she eyed the bathroom tile. Taking a step back, she gave no outward sign of trouble to come. Not so much as a grin or a smirk did she paint on her face and then, stepping aside to let Anna pass, it happened. There was a sound and a movement behind her, though before Anna's senses could react a shock of pain hit her in the back causing her to drop to the floor. As she tried to raise her upper body, she opened her eyes to see a pair of purple leather cowboy boots stepping forward. The pointed toe thrust into her stomach. She couldn't breathe—the effort to pull breath into herself was frightening. Clenching her stomach Anna laid on her side, nauseated, feeling the horrible reflex sensation of vomit grip her. Then, the sound of hard heels blended with a rush of music. It was faintly heard and then it was gone.

The devil hovered over Anna's body

"Stupidity becomes you, you dumb bitch," Mrs. Barker laughed.

Anna could scarcely make out two fat feet that were screaming to escape petite shoes. One shoe moved and Anna cried out in pain again, clenching her stomach tighter. The squishing of nylons came closer, and upon the side of her face a mouthful of spit landed. The sound of feet finally moved away.

Mrs. Barker paused at the door. "Let this be a reminder to you of *who I am* and *what* I am capable of. Never, ever underestimate me again!" The door made a whoosh sound as it shut behind her.

~*~

Making his way around the room, James did not see Anna sitting down, and much to his relief, he did not see her dancing with another man. Desperately needing fresh air, he headed for the exit, hoping to find Anna waiting for him there, but she was not. In the distance, two red lights sped down the road and disappeared into the night.

The air felt good on his face and neck as he loosened his tie and stretched his neck from side to side. He would cool off awhile, breathe in the sweet evening air, and admire the beautiful harvest moon before going back in to find Anna.

Suddenly, the door behind him opened, but the footsteps on the porch were not soft and quiet as Anna's would be.

"Here he is!"

James turned to see Anna's father holding the open door and her mother quickly coming down the steps.

"Pastor Edwards, I'm glad we found you—have you seen Anna?" she asked in nearly one breath.

He could not help but notice the worried look on their faces, and a strange feeling washed over his body.

"No, but I was just about to go in and look for her myself."

"There is buzz going around the room," Mrs. McManus continued, "that a girl was seen doubled over and in tears at the back of this building a while ago, and we can't find Anna!"

James looked out into the black night where just a few minutes ago he had seen taillights disappearing down the road, and he knew.

His mouth opened, and for a brief moment no words

would form as James felt adrenaline seizing him. Without looking at Anna's parents he blurted out, "Don't leave here. Don't leave!" And then he ran.

He left the bewildered and anxious parents standing on the sidewalk in front of the Social Hall without further explanation. They watched the young pastor quickly get into his truck and the red taillights disappear down the road and into the darkness. They put their arms around each other. Inwardly they knew that whatever was wrong, it would be best to stay at the dance a while longer.

The truck's accelerator needle rapidly swung to the right as James pushed the pedal to the floor in his flight to the McManus house. Why would Anna—if it *was* her, be in tears out behind the building? Someone had to have done or said something terrible to her—*if* it was her. He had a lot of questions he wanted to ask. For a long time now he had wanted to know who those two men were and what they did to her after she spoke of them that dreary February morning in the McManus barn.

Memory had not forgotten other words that were spoken that were not so harsh. At the time, he had had no right to ask just who those individuals were. Particularly the one who lay in the earth's crust. He did not truly know Anna. He did not know the extent of her soul and its vast personality that he had unknowingly stepped upon during his first sermon.

It was her music and the depth she took it to that he had difficulty understanding. As a musician himself, he understood the passion a musician possesses when they play. Their instrument is a part of themselves where the mind and soul becomes one and is taken to a higher level of consciousness. Surrounded within a euphoric blissfulness, James had spent hour after hour lingering over the keys, totally unaware of the world around him. He had no doubt in his mind that she was part of that very special world. But there was something else.

It was as if the violin was her only source of *real* security. She guarded it with her life because it probably was the only thing that *hadn't* hurt her, and it was driving him crazy knowing that her life was probably common knowledge to everyone except him. Anna never directly volunteered any information about her past, and because of this, he never asked.

The McManus house, which usually had just about every light on at night, sat somewhere off to his left as he slowed the truck and entered the long dirt driveway. Not a single bulb was lit, and even with the light of the moon the mood was eerie.

Anna's old truck was parked a short distance away from the house, and slowly pulling up next to it, he turned off the ignition. From where he stood, he could see a dark figure on the porch and walking slowly towards it, the sound of sobbing became evident. James found her sitting on the porch against the house, her knees bent with arms resting on them, and her arms cradling her head. In a moment he was next to her.

"Anna, what happened?" he asked, resting a hand on her back.

She did not answer him.

"Anna, for God's sake, tell me what happened. Please?"

She lifted her head off her arms, and James noticed

something different in her expression, or the lack of. Part of her was missing. Her eyes seemed oddly vacant as she sat there, staring at nothing. She still hadn't looked at him yet, but he felt she wasn't completely avoiding him. Then a puzzled looked crossed her features as if she were trying to figure something out.

"James," she said at last, "All my life I have considered myself a strong person, but she took me by surprise. Of all people, she took me by surprise." Her voice trailed off. Keeping her eyes lowered, she whispered, "She said that I...was stupid. I'm not, am I?"

He reached for her face and lifted it gently.

"Look at me, Anna. *Look* at me."

With some reluctance, her tear-stained eyes cautiously brought themselves to meet his, but she wanted to avoid them, for they were filled with questions that she didn't want him to ask.

"Anna McManus, you tell me *right now* who did this!"

She paused and slowly shook her head.

"I'm sorry James—I can't. I underestimated her. . .and I paid the price."

"What are you saying?" James nearly growled in frustration.

Anna let out a sigh.

"I had forgotten what she could do to me. Tonight was a reminder."

"This is garbage!" James was beyond impatient and tightened his hands on Anna's face, but he saw that fear was quickly rising in her and he found himself wrapping his arms around her.

"I'm sorry, I'm sorry!" James shut his eyes tight and buried his face into her neck, into her soft hair, and again he found himself wanting to protect this woman that was so near to him. What price did she pay for underestimating whom? James made a silent vow to the woman he was holding, that he would find out who *she* was and when he did, he would punish her in retaliation for past injuries. As the opening to his heart widened with compassion, its chambers were also filled with a strong desire for revenge; and so strong was this feeling that it took precedence over forgiveness.

Having lifted her head off his shoulder, Anna quietly murmured, "Look at the moon now. I bet you don't see that in Seattle."

James stood up and offered his hands to her, and standing side by side on the worn porch, they looked at the glowing orange moon.

"It's so close that you or I could reach right out and touch it if we wanted to. I only wish harvest moons would come to visit more often," Anna whispered.

"There is one way," James suggested, "but you must watch very carefully."

He held an imaginary jar in his hand, and holding it up to the huge orange moon, he poked it down into the jar with a finger, and then carefully screwed on a lid.

"From me, to you, as a remembrance of this night."

Anna accepted his gift and thanked him, but he told her to put it down on the railing, for there was one more thing to be done in order to make the evening complete. He took her into his arms and waited for her to hold onto him.

"But where is the music?" she asked.

"Shh. . .listen, just listen," he whispered.

Anna closed her eyes and listened to the night that consisted of nothing more than a few moths fluttering against the screen door, and while she embraced the feel of the hushed world around them, the low moan of a faraway train whistle blew its haunting yet placid sound over the moonlit farmland.

"Now I do," she quietly announced, wrapping her left hand around the back of his neck.

James was too aware of her soft body against his, her curving waist and hips that his hands were touching. He wanted to take her and lay her down and make love to her. But his own words resurfaced in his mind and he shut his eyes tight against them, but they washed away his will and came anyway. "I never want to hurt you, and I made a promise to you. Nothing more, nothing less. Nothing less, nothing more."

He had stopped moving and was holding her tightly. A long silence hung in the air. He wanted to savor it, to hold the moment in time forever.

Her presence was his strength. She was the source of his inspiration, the calm spirit that fed his inner being each day. When there seemed to be no other listening ear, it was Anna who was the river of comfort that flowed continuously in his life.

Nature was beckoning and prepared to sweep a hand over the two mellowing hearts. A gentle breeze came off the rolling hills and played through the blades of tall, dry grass. In the nearby trees, it caused leaves to sway. The autumn sky bent down to touch the hilltops of gold, and upon the faint breeze words were whispered to the trees.

What more could they do?

His senses were not blind, for he had heard the nudging of nature. And yes, he agreed that he was holding a precious gift, one that may be given just once in a lifetime. But the time was not right. Not yet.

Her head was bowed, and Anna did not look up to meet his, which was bowed too.

"I think—it would be best if I left now," James barely whispered. Anna could only smile a small smile with closed lips and little nod.

He slowly turned toward his truck but was having trouble keeping his feet moving in that direction. The night was coming to a close but it didn't feel right—something was missing and he knew what it was and he wanted it badly. James suddenly stopped.

Anna had called out his name and upon turning around he saw her reach into her dress pocket and take out the old dance card. Until now, he had forgotten all about it, but she hadn't.

"Thank you, for this. I'll remember tonight as long as there's a harvest moon. . .*wherever* I am."

Coming back to her, he carefully folded her fingers around the card, cupping his hands over hers.

"Thank you, for allowing me to enjoy your company. I'll *always* remember tonight, even when there's no harvest moon."

She looked so beautiful standing there, drenched in the light from the sky, that he found himself kissing her forehead. His lips stayed upon her warm skin, but it was not her forehead he wanted to kiss. Her lips were too close to be ignored; they looked too warm, too soft.

He shut his eyes against the agony.

He had to do it now. He had to keep his eyes shut while turning away. He wanted to say goodnight, but he kept his mouth still. And as he got into his truck and started it, he forced himself to look at the steering wheel, to concentrate on the lights ahead of him that were drawing him down the uneven driveway. When the tires touched the main road, he allowed himself to look into the rear view mirror and saw only blackness there. It was then that he realized, he had held his breath almost the entire length of the dirt driveway.

~*~

Anna wrapped her arms around one of the white columns on the porch while watching his truck rise and fall over the gently rolling land. At last her eyes could hardly make out the taillights, and then he was gone from view. As she lingered there, it was impossible to ignore the awesome sight that hung miles above her.

Anna went back into the quiet house. In the kitchen pantry she found one of her empty jelly jars with a lid and seal, and standing on the front porch, she put the dance card in the jar. She began to hold the jar up, but she stopped and removed the card and opened it to the last page. On the last line inscribed in his handwriting were the words,

HARVEST MOON
*Thank You,*
*James Michael Edwards*

Anna's fingers were on her lips as she read the words again and again. She sighed deeply and put her hand on her chest. She kissed her fingertips, and touching his words, she put the dance card back in the glass jar. She held the jar above her head until it was aligned with the moon, and then the moon and the dance card were sealed with the lid. The two would have much to talk about within the confines of their new home.

They presently left the porch and were carried upstairs to her room. The light from the sky was the only light permitted in her room as she undressed for bed. On the nightstand under the window, they watched her sit on the edge of the bed as the curtains lifted in the breeze.

Eventually, the orange moon turned white.

Slipping under the covers, she reached out for the jar of memories that joined her on the pillow for the rest of the night.

## CHAPTER 8—AUTHOR OF RUMORS

In less than half an hour, his congregation would be occupying the space that he quietly took up on that first Sunday of October. The morning sun greeted him through stained glass windows to his right and James wondered, while basking in the colored warmth, how many other pastors had sat there since the church was built in 1912. He breathed deep, for sentimentality had seized his heart, and contentment ran rampant through his body.

Pastor James Edwards sat in the third pew on the left side of the little church. He had chosen to sit in the McManus pew. One reason was that he wanted to claim kinship with the family. After he and Anna had settled in after the "peace treaty," he felt as if he belonged more to their family than he did to his own. This was, for the most part, due to the persistence of Polly McManus that he should join them every Sunday for a home-cooked meal.

It would be hard to explain to another how much he looked forward to feeling like he was part of a *normal* family. They treated him as though he were one of them. James eyed the rest of the church pew where soon they would gather.

The thought of having a family of his own had become a subject of interest to his mind on more than one occasion.

His stomach let out a faint growl, and remembering that it was only fed toast and coffee for breakfast, he told it to behave itself during the service. In a few hours he would be feasting on another delicious meal. Anna had called him the day before to ask if he liked pot roast and apple pie—as if she had to ask. The McManus women should have known by now that he ate anything that was put before him. James' mouth began to water at the thought of food.

In a few hours, while waiting for more than just the aroma from supper to be served, teenagers would surround him. To keep his mind off his suffering he would tell a story or a joke. More often than not Mrs. McManus stepped out of the kitchen, assuming a child of hers was acting inappropriately in front of company. Little did she suspect that it was her dear pastor who was the culprit who started the jokes. When their mother returned to the kitchen, the kids would burst out laughing while he gave them a wink.

He hoped that the McManus kids would think of him in a different way besides just being their pastor. James hoped that if they ever needed to talk to him, they would. Not because he was their pastor, but because he was their friend.

While his thoughts shifted from the younger kids to their oldest sister, his heart took pleasure in the satisfaction of knowing the most important reason. He laid a hand on his leg and envisioned her small yet very strong hand under his. His warm flesh would cover hers as they sat in the pew listening to the organist practice before services. He could be her husband, and she could be his wife. They would each be holding a child in their arms while another was growing inside her womb.

He bowed his head, closed his eyes, and folded his hands in prayer. James thanked God for the beautiful morning, his new life, his many friends, but most of all he thanked God for one person in particular.

With much reluctance, James removed himself from the pew and made his way up the two steps and into the vestibule. The air was a little stuffy so the door facing the parking lot was opened a bit. After slipping his vestment over his head, James heard the sound of shoes on the sidewalk, a woman's voice, and then another. He paused. The women stopped just outside the vestibule door, carrying on their conversation as if they were oblivious to where they were or of the possibility that he could be inside the little room listening to their every word. James knew he should not be eavesdropping, but what could he do? The women had placed themselves there.

"I think Regina—I mean *Faith*—has gone too far this time."

"Yes, I'm afraid you're right."

"I was shocked at what she was telling us during our last visit with her."

The second woman added, "I quite didn't know

what to say. We should have said *something.* It was
our *duty* to defend those not present."

"Yes, I know. I feel awful about it now. Knowing
Regina the way we do, the news probably has spread
past Dusty and throughout the Palouse!"

There was a moment or two of silence.

"Ever since the Harvest Dance, she has been so
giddy about Pastor Edwards taking an interest in her
daughter . . ."

A hand quickly flew to cup his mouth, and James
hoped the two women didn't hear a repulsed laugh
coming from inside the vestibule.

"I do feel sorry for her poor daughter," continued
the first lady. "If she had *any* backbone, she wouldn't
let her mother turn her into—*her.*"

"Well, if there's anyone to feel sorry for it's her
husband, poor thing." The second lady sighed
sympathetically. "Have you ever seen Regina—I mean
*Faith,* kick him when he's trying to sing? Bless his poor
heart."

"Poor thing? He should have wondered why he was
husband number four!"

"*If* he was told at all!"

James could almost hear the first lady shaking her
head. "Well, I do pity him, I guess, but he isn't the one
we should be worried about. Things have been said
about our good neighbor which I *know* can't be true.
I've known Richard McManus forever, and I don't think
he's the kind of man who would give a piece of his land
away to a man willing to take Anna off his hands." She
stopped for breath. "How did Regina put it? 'A good
piece of farming land could be acquired from the father

on the condition that the spinster daughter be taken in marriage. Love not required in the agreement.'" She continued, in indignation, "No, I know Richard better than that. Of all the ridiculous things I've ever heard! Anna is no beauty, but she has more personality, wit, and intelligence than most girls I know. That includes, I'm sorry to say, my own granddaughter's."

The second lady observed, "I wouldn't mind having her for a granddaughter myself."

"Did you notice what a nice couple Pastor Edwards and Anna made at the dance?"

"I did see, and so did Regina. If there was ever a hymn of hate, that woman's face sang it! It just wasn't Christian. Just wasn't!"

The first lady sighed. "That woman has never gotten over her loss, and for some reason I can't understand she blames Anna."

"But it wasn't the girl's fault."

"I know that, you know that, and everyone else knows that. I wouldn't be surprised if she tried to convince God himself to have a biased opinion in the matter! She really has twisted denial to be her reality."

The second lady concurred. "And after all these years, her warped conscience must be having a field day."

"That poor girl has been through *enough*. A lesser woman would have lost her constitution completely. She has had to find comfort and strength in something, or else she's very good in the postponement of suffering."

James could hear both women sigh heavily.

"Well, I suppose we better go in and take our seats."

"Oh, just to let you know, if you're fixing on having the pastor over for dinner, don't make liver and onions."

"Definitely not?"

"Definitely not. Last time we had him over, he just ate the peas, the pie, and the pumpkin bread."

The two women laughed and their voices faded away.

On the other side of the door, a man stood unmoved. James was too numb and too filled with rage to move. How could he go out there when he did not trust his own temper? How could he go out there and face everyone when he could see a snake in the grass? A snake? The Serpent? The *Serpent*. His blood ran cold.

James pressed his eyes shut and asked God—no, he *begged* God to give him wisdom and strength. His lips began to whisper parts of Psalms 144 and 145.

"Part your heavens, O Lord, and come down;
touch the mountains, so that they smoke.
Send forth lightning and scatter the enemies;
shoot your arrows and rout them.
Reach down your hand from on high;
deliver me and rescue me
from the mighty water,
from the hands of foreigners
whose mouths are full of lies,
whose right hands are deceitful."
The Lord is near to all who call on Him,
to all who call on Him in truth.
He fulfills the desires of those who fear Him;
He hears their cry and saves them.
The Lord watches over all who love Him,

but all the wicked He will destroy."

After closing the vestibule door behind him, James approached the pulpit but did not make eye contact with the members below. He fixed his stare on one of the stained glass windows and continued to do so in the uncomfortable growing silence. By now, everyone had reason to believe that this Sunday was proving to be quite different from the usual.

His little flock grew nervous and stole short glances at each other. Among the concerned were Anna and her family, and when they turned to her with questioning looks, she shrugged her shoulders.

At last their dear pastor breathed deeply and they waited for his eyes to fall on them, which would be followed by a warm smile and a "Good morning, everyone!" Instead, he seemed to be captivated by the brightness of the stained glass windows and his mind seemed to be somewhere else.

They did not know, nor could know, how crucial the morning sun was as a distraction to keep him from looking down and into the eyes of the enemy. When his eyes were finally a blur, he began.

"Our Creator is the Author of Life, and each of us is the author of our own lives. But there is an author that I would not want to be known for. You folks have heard me tell stories in lieu of sermons, and this morning will be no different."

Pastor Edwards continued, "In the Jewish religion, gossip is looked upon as a terrible sin. And so, the story begins of a young man giving grief to this Elder who was considered wise. The young man would go about town spreading lies about the Elder, until one day the

Elder had had enough. He scolded the young man.

"'How can I be forgiven?' the young man finally asked. The Elder said, 'First, take this bag of feathers, go to the mountain top and empty it.'

"'That is all?' asked the young man. 'That is all,' the Elder replied.

"And so the young man did as he was told, and all the feathers were cast in all directions by the wind. Upon reaching the town where the Elder waited, the young man said, 'I have done what you asked. Am I forgiven now?'

"'Not yet. You must do one more thing.' 'What is it?' asked the young man.

"'Go and pick up all of the feathers.' 'But that would be impossible to get them all back!' 'And so are the words that were spoken against me.'"

A long silence followed while James bent his head and folded his hands.

"My dear friends, I speak not for myself, but for two very good friends which may have been injured due to a loose tongue. I asked that you pray very hard to our loving God above, that He may forgive the Author of Rumors."

With his head still bowed, Pastor Edwards slowly turned away from the pulpit and closed the vestibule door behind him.

The congregation, confused and bewildered, sat wide-eyed and silent. At last, a male voice from the McManus family rose above a whisper.

"So what do we do *now*?"

"Looks like we get to go home a little early," one of the sisters announced as she noticed folks closest to the back door quietly slipping out.

"Well, that was different," Mr. McManus admitted as he rose from his seat. Looking down at his eldest daughter, he casually inquired, "Anna, is there anything that *you* would like to tell us?"

"Why are you looking at *me*?"

"Oh, let's just say that I've seen something like this before," he suggested with a humorous grin.

"Sorry Dad, I didn't have a hand in this one. But I *do* have to give Pastor Edwards credit."

"Do I dare ask?"

"Well, it's obvious isn't it? His little production was *far* better than mine."

"Let's go home everyone," Mrs. McManus announced. "Your mother needs to get cooking a pot roast and apple pie for a *very* upset pastor. On second thought, I better make two pies, 'cause upset men tend to be hungry men."

Slipping her arms in the sleeves of the coat her husband held for her, she worked at the buttons and huffed, "Men!"

## CHAPTER 9—THE QUIET MAN

Although it was November 5th, the weather behaved as if September were taking a last bow before the early winter months cloaked the landscape in frost, hardened the earth, and finally spread a blanket of winter's white.

At the moment, James sat contentedly in the early evening sun on his front porch steps. His coffee cup, although empty, rested in his warm hands as his arms leaned on his jeans-covered knees. He glanced down at his right knee where the material was worn and ripped, exposing a few inches of skin. A little smile moved his lips as happiness filled him while he thought of Anna.

James could almost feel her sitting next to him on his right, as she always did. Anna did not need to be physically by his side in order for her to be there. At times, he found himself talking to her. It was during difficult hours of writing his sermons that he would talk to her from across the little kitchen table. Her cup would be filled, the handle facing right, her chair pulled out.

He found himself still smiling as he glanced down at his comfortable torn jeans. He was remembering a quiet moment a few weeks ago when her hand cautiously touched his leg and lightly made its way onto his knee. He remembered how her fingertips slowly ran back and forth on his skin. He couldn't forget her hand resting there. He hadn't forgotten how she let her hand go slowly back up his leg. He had fixed his eyes on Anna's face, and as he took her hand into both of his, she turned her head away from him. The rising pink in her checks did not go unnoticed.

She would not look at him, so he brought her hand close to his lips and kept it there for a moment or two. Still, she would not meet his eyes, so James brought her hand to his lips and kissed it. Her eyes were shut tight, and anguish briefly crossed her face while he kept her hand upon his mouth. His eyes were fixed upon hers, searching for a vein of affection. He wanted—and needed—more than the lukewarm, physical restraint that she was allowed to offer him. His eyes questioned hers which, with all their strength, were trying to avoid his.

"Please do me the favor of closing your eyes," Anna quietly requested. "Do not open them, or you'll only have my memory to keep you company."

Unwillingly, James closed his eyes, and without saying a word, released her hand and let his hands rest in his lap. There was a slight sound as Anna got up from the steps. All was still for a moment or two, and he was afraid that his eyes would open—even though his willpower told them not to. It was then that he felt her warm lips touch his forehead. He felt her breath upon his skin. His heartbeat and his flesh moved. James breathed deeply and spoke her name when the agony became too much. Anna's warmth and softness lifted from his skin and then he heard her footsteps back away.

When he allowed his eyes to open, she was on the road heading home.

His maleness had reason to stir, for the Lord of Creation must have taken into consideration for the union of male and female; the allurement, the temptation, the thirst, the craving, the yearning of flesh and blood urgently and ambitiously devoted to feel the want of *wanting*, the first Eve.

James was anxious and feared the collapse of their "nothing more, nothing less" friendship would come from his own doing. He tried to think about something else and decided to carry out an observation of the sun that was no longer hot and intense. It was tired and was lowering itself upon the earth, casting long shadows, leaning them sharply away from buildings and trees. The time had passed for the sun to give up its uncomfortable July and August temperatures as James found comfort and refreshment in the new season.

A cool, rippling breeze brushed his face, and closing his eyes, he filled his lungs with the sweet country air around him. The gentle breeze skimmed against his face over and over until it was Anna's hands that he felt upon his skin. His own hands reached up and covered hers.

James Edwards agreed, without any reservations,

that he was a happy man who spent a portion of his day sitting on his porch steps that faced gentle rolling land that was home—his home.

Just two months' shy of a year, he couldn't believe how fast time had passed since he said goodbye to Seattle. As he thought of the big city with Puget Sound in its front yard, he did not ache for it as he had months ago. It would be nice, he often thought, to take Anna there and show her the Space Needle and the waterfront, then take a ferryboat ride as the powerful steel vessel frothed and churned the salty, cold water in its wake. There were a lot of things that he loved about the city, but he did not feel as if part of him were still there.

Opening his eyes, he let them run over the fields that had been harvested months ago. They had been good to the farmers, and the earth was praised and blessed. Nothing more would be asked of her until spring. For now, she could rest and turn bleak as winter approached.

If he hadn't done so already, James was beginning to wonder if he was understanding and admiring this land. When he thought of all the seasons during his life, none meant more to him than those during the past ten months. It would be hard to imagine what his life would be like now, without Anna. She had ever so slowly crept into his thoughts, into his body, into his heart. He had no intention ten months ago of ever wanting to know, much less be alone with her in her father's little café. Time and circumstances had changed his heart, and now he couldn't imagine what he would do if Anna were taken from him.

An involuntary shiver shook his body, and the

horrible thought was not given a chance to even consider the possibility. Picking himself off the steps, James went back into the kitchen and poured more coffee. Glancing out the window above the little table, he decided that there was enough time for a short walk before dusk set in. As he placed a hand on the screen door, he caught sight of a woman coming up his driveway on foot. She had her head down and was wiping her eyes. Her shoulders leaned forward and were shaking. And in her right hand she held something that was hard to make out from behind the screen door. Putting the coffee down on the nearest end table, he slowly closed the door behind him. He went down the few steps and stopped as Anna came toward the house. She moved toward him and stopped a short distance away, tears running down her face. Opening his arms, Anna quickly rushed into them. Her tears ran down his shirt until his skin was cold. Little by little her sobbing lessened.

He led her into the house and sat down on the sofa beside her. He put an arm around her as she leaned back against him, her head on his shoulder. James glanced down at her lap and found a man's cap clenched in her hands, and wondered whom it belonged to. Anna was home early from the café and suddenly he thought that something may have happened to her friend Curly, but he didn't recall Curly ever wearing caps.

James looked down at Anna and she had her eyes closed. Her head felt nice against him, and she didn't seem to care if there wasn't any distance between their bodies. He knew that she would talk to him after some time had passed so he took the opportunity to rest his head upon hers, and couldn't have asked for anything more in the hushed, silence.

Finally, he asked if she wanted coffee, but she shook her head. She was offered a glass of wine, but shook her head again and moved to the edge of the couch.

"The quiet man died today," she managed to whisper.

James sighed and leaned forward to get a better look at the cap. It was old and stained, and Anna kept looking at it with inconsolable sadness and bewilderment.

"I had put his cap on," she began, trying to control the quivering in her voice, "and then he told me to keep it. I . . . I told him that he wouldn't look the same without it." Anna was quiet for a moment. "He looked at me with the strangest expression on his face and said that he wouldn't be needing it much longer. He thanked me for being kind to him over the years, and right after that, he grabbed his chest, fell off the stool, hit the floor, and was—dead."

Anna got up from the couch and walked around the room. "In all the years I've waited on him, that was the most he ever said to me."

"Did he have a name?"

She turned to him in disbelief, then snapped, "Yes James, he did!" She went over to the living room window and looked out and saw the light leaving the day, and her reflection almost lived in the glass. "His name was Harry."

"Harry. Harry what?"

Anger was building in her eyes, and her

eyebrows narrowed.

"That was it! We just knew him as Harry. His name was—Harry!" She started sniffling and James thought another cry was coming on. But she turned around and looked at him.

"How could he say that I was kind to him when I didn't even know his last name? I asked Curly if he knew, but he didn't even know. I thought Curly knew everything about everyone who spent time in the café."

James said softly, "Maybe Harry just wanted to be in the company of others, and know that he could feel at home without folks wanting to know all about him."

James saw her head bend forward and she crossed her arms under her chest. He got up and stood behind her, looking at their dim images against the front window.

"But he shouldn't have died without folks not knowing his last name," she whispered to her faint reflection.

James remained puzzled. "Why is that so important to you?"

She moved away from him, sitting on the piano bench, shaking her head in disapproval at him.

"You just don't understand, do you?" she snapped accusingly.

James rubbed his forehead with his fingers. "I'm *trying*, but I can't see what's under that skull of yours. So please, do me a favor, Anna, and brief me on what I do not understand. And while you're at it, just remember that it wasn't me who carried out the death sentence on Harry. Like it or not, death happens. It's hell for the people who see it and are left behind. But when we wake up each morning, we know that God had granted us another day to be part of the living."

Anna huffed. "And everyone acts like it's a forever thing, but living is just temporary. Dying is permanent." She paused for a moment. "Don't you ever get the feeling that God is up there shuffling a big deck of cards, and just maybe, at any moment, he'll draw one with your name on it? I guess I wouldn't care if I was really old, but to die young, to be plucked off of this earth at any moment, without warning . . . *that* is what scares the hell out of me!"

James couldn't help but notice her worried eyes and ashen skin.

She said passionately, "When I die, I want my soul to fly into a killdeer bird, so I may live on earth just a little while longer. I would rather die inside my favorite bird and dissolve into the wheat fields, than be counted among corpses in box tombs."

*Dissolve.* James wanted to correct her and say that animals don't dissolve—they decompose, rot, and then the maggots—his guts squirmed at the thought. *Bite your tongue, James*, he told himself. *She knows that. She lives on a farm. She's seen it for herself.*

He continued, "Anna, you have to make plans to live forever . . ."

She shook her head.

He leaned forward and asked gently, "And why not?"

Her answer did not come right away. She lifted her eyes to his and told him honestly, "I don't trust life to let me live forever."

There was nothing he wanted to say or could say to

that. He quickly noticed the cap and changed the subject.

"I'm glad Harry thought well enough of you to give you his special possession."

She glanced at the cap while James sat down beside her on the piano bench. In a low voice he added, "You know, not every man gives his hat away."

Her chest rose and fell, and her lips formed a slight smile. He lowered his head to her ear and whispered, "But I suppose you know that."

"I do, but thanks for saying so."

"You're welcome."

"It was just so weird." Anna twisted her hands together as she remembered. "Someone was pushing down on his chest, and someone else was blowing his breath into Harry's corpse. Another person got on the phone and called for help, but I knew it was all in vain." She paused. "I knew—I just *knew* that he was gone even before the medics arrived. Death has a look of its own, and I wanted to let the medics know that the quiet man was gone. Gone for good. They were wasting their time on a dead man. While they were doing their duty, they gave me a half-second glance without stopping CPR. But later on, while driving away from the cafe, I bet they said to one another, 'She knew. She *knew*, didn't she?'

"It was just so eerie knowing that his guardian angel led his soul away from us sometime after his body crumpled on the floor. The medics finally admitted that there was nothing else they could do for Harry. His skin had been turning shades of blue, purple, and tomb white. Life was reversed and covered the body in a shade of whitish gray before a pure white cloth did not allow us to see Harry anymore."

Anna handed the old, worn cap to James so he could observe it himself.

"Nearly all the older male customers I know want their hats or caps placed upon their chests with their hands folded over them while they lie in eternal rest. They don't want to wear a suit. Those bits of clothing, they told me, wouldn't say a thing about who they were. Out here, a man may have been wearing a hat or cap since boyhood."

Anna sighed. "I suppose these things have seen it all. Triumphs and failures, the good and the bad." She paused long enough to take back Harry's cap. "My dad still has his father's hat. Mom says he puts it on once a year, on the day his father died. I'm not supposed to know, so I keep my mouth shut about it."

"Do you take after your father in any way?" James asked.

While she thought how to answer him, the quiet house seemed to patiently wait for her reply.

"In our own way, we both have this yearning to bring back people we loved, or would like to have known. Whether it's dad wearing his father's hat, or myself, carrying on a tradition of music my grandfather and great-grandfather loved."

She added thoughtfully, "We have a picture of my dad's folks, and they're standing by an old Essex car, and I wondered what ever happened to it. And as I wondered, there was a look of despair, hardship, and barrenness that was all around them as they stood in the dust of the Great Depression."

She shook her head fiercely. "I am bitter and furious at the North Dakota prairie for the cruelty it inflicted upon them. It's not hard to see why no one is smiling. They lost a son, they lost their farm, and they lost a way of life that was all they knew. I can imagine that one of Grandpa's few pleasures that hadn't been taken from him was his love for the violin."

Recalling, she mused, "I was twelve when my Grandpa died. I wish that we could have known each other better. I'm almost sorry for having been young and ignorant of others around me. But I don't know if he would have talked about his life, even if I had thought to ask him."

After mulling it over for a moment, Anna shook her head. "No, I don't think he would have. I can see him leaning back in his easy chair, taking his pipe from his mouth, and giving me one of his hard stares while offering me a piece of butterscotch candy." Anna smiled a little and chuckled.

"I wonder if he had any idea how earthshaking his silent stares were to a kid? I wonder if he knew that I saw him as a quiet, distant figure who belonged more to my father than to me? Another 'quiet man,' like Harry.

Anna straightened her spine and pushed her shoulders back. Her chin lifted and it appeared as if some object across the room was worthy of her stare.

"So, that's how it has to be. When we cannot be with those who are no longer here, we pick up the pieces and try to salvage what they lost. We hope—I hope, that somehow they hear us and are proud of what we are doing."

James added thoughtfully, "And that the next

generation will never forget you. That they honor your life and memory in their own way."

Anna was quiet while James turned around and faced the black and ivory keys.

"Do you think they *will*?" Her question was spoken as if she thought the dead might hear her, her words strained with worry and doubt.

His fingertips softly and slowly echoed the mood of the evening. "If they are anything like you, they will. They *will*."

## CHAPTER 10—THE GUEST

The door to the café opened, and along with a nip of cold air, a stranger came in the day before Thanksgiving.

On both sides of the door were signs reminding customers that the café would be closed Thanksgiving Day, but would be open the next. As he quietly closed the door, the sign lifted up from the bottom just a bit and settled back. At the bottom of the paper were two words: "Thanks, Anna."

He let out a long sigh, for his drive had been a long and lonely one. He smiled wearily, for he knew he had come to the right place. His warm overcoat slipped off his shoulders and he hung it by its sheepskin collar on the coat stand next to the door. Any observer would assume he was a regular customer as the man casually slid onto the only available stool at the counter.

The newcomer did not attract much attention, for it was the noon hour and the warm air in the little café was filled with a constant hum of chatter. The three men on his left and the one on his right nodded to the stranger, but did not start a conversation with him. What they did not know was that he was not terribly fond of engaging in conversations with strangers. He was a man who observed and took in his surroundings, and firmly believed that God gave Adam and Eve language to be used sparingly. He watched a young woman dressed in blue jeans, cream-yellow T-shirt, white shoes and a small apron as she swooshed around from table to table.

The waitress quickly came to the counter area and clipped three notes of paper to the wheel and whirled it in the cook's direction. Her finger dinged the chrome bell sharply on the shiny counter next to the waiting plates.

Loud and clear her voice was heard throughout the busy café: "Twelve-twelve and all's well!"

Along the length of her left arm, four plates were artfully balanced while she carried the fifth in her right hand. As she turned away from him to deliver the lunches, she threw a few words behind her that his presence had not gone unnoticed and that he would not be forgotten in the rush. Before him was a brown coffee cup turned upside down on a saucer, and reaching out for it, he turned it over, making a slight clink upon the saucer. He straightened the silverware on the waiting napkin. With this task done, he joined his hands together on the counter and patiently waited.

The waitress wore a flush of pink in her cheeks and wiped her forehead as she emptied dirty dishes somewhere under the countertop. With the smoothest of movements, she lifted a half-empty glass coffee pot from one heated burner to another. Emptying the old coffee grounds, she inserted a clean filter, poured in fresh grounds, filled the machine with water, hit a button and put the glass pot under the coffee that began to drip and sizzle on the hot burner.

Grabbing the half-empty pot, she worked her way down the counter refilling cups, putting dirty dishes under the counter, and slipping pieces of paper next to almost-finished meals. Turning in his direction, she tiredly filled his cup and then said that she would take his order in just a second.

"That's all right," he assured her, "I'm in no hurry."

Once more she went through the routine of making more coffee. Finally, she turned around, and while reaching for her pad and pen, she glanced down as she thanked the customer for his patience. But as her eyes lifted to his face, she held the pad and pen in mid-air and stared at the man who wore a gentle grin, sitting quietly with his hands folded together.

"Good afternoon," he said, nodding to her.

She was looking at him in a way that made him think that she was trying to figure something out.

"I'm sorry, but I feel as if we've met before," she said.

"Have we?"

"I don't know," she said as she smiled back, the puzzled look still twinkling in her eyes, "but while I'm thinking of where, can I get you something to eat?"

"By any chance, can I still get breakfast?"

"Breakfast? Well, we usually don't serve it at this hour 'cause cook has everything geared for lunch."

"I understand. I shouldn't have mentioned it except—well, I hear that your raspberry syrup is wonderful over French toast. It would be a treat after coming this far."

"May I ask where 'far' is?"

"Seattle."

"Ah, yes, *Seattle*." She narrowed his eyebrows as she studied his eyes. She bent closer to him and whispered, "You look familiar. I feel as if I *should* know you."

Raising the coffee to his lips, he paused for a moment and thought for an answer, but took a slow swallow instead.

"Good coffee."

The man sitting to the right of the stranger glanced over at him and spoke over the rim of his cup as he was just about to take a swallow.

"Anna, just give the man his damn breakfast. Imagine, coming all the way from Seattle. Now if that ain't a compliment, I don't know what is!"

"Roy! Behave yourself." Anna grinned at him.

The man looked up at the waitress and looked surprised at the mention of his name.

"*What*?"

"Oh!" She was shooing him with the back of her hand and shaking her head at him. "Finish your lunch before I throw you out."

The man laughed. "It wouldn't be the first time!" He braced himself for a smack on the head, but the young woman laughed with him instead and smiled as she wrote on her pad. She turned away and put the order on the spinning wheel and said to the cook, "French stack with plenty of Razzle Dazzle!"

She hit the bell again and said, "'Tis twelve-twenty, and tomorrow Tom Turkey is coming to town with tuckers on his toes. Eat, drink, and be merry everyone, this is a great time to be alive! "It 'tis, it 'tis!" she chanted in a mock accent.

One by one, the booths and stools became vacant, and the little café was much quieter. Tables and counter tops were wiped down, and the rag was folded and placed beside the coffee machines while the stranger mopped up every drop of the raspberry syrup. He glanced around him and saw that he was the only customer left. The tired-looking waitress brought a pot of coffee over to him. Holding it poised over his cup she asked, "More?"

"Only if you'll have some with me."

She grinned with relief and sighed. Pouring a cup for herself, she took up the seat on his left.

Making conversation, she inquired, "So, are you visiting someone tomorrow, or are you running away from someone?" The waitress did not look at him, as she was too exhausted, so the stranger turned his head briefly to look at her.

He turned his eyes back to his cup and said, "A little bit of both."

She let out a small sigh. "Well now, you're the second person from Seattle I know who is running away from someone."

As he sat beside the young woman who was rubbing her shoulders with equally weary hands, he found himself opening up to her, and probably had said too much already. This was unusual for him to talk so much—especially to a woman. For as long as he could recall, he had been a quiet man who spoke few words. In his estimation, this did not seem to bother the world too much, because it kept on spinning and did not take much notice of him. And that suited him just fine.

Except for today.

"Has this *other* person stopped running?" he asked.

"It seems as if he has."

"What makes you so sure?"

"Well, when he first came here, compared to now—what a difference."

The man was intrigued. "How so?"

The young woman thought for a few moments and finally offered, "He reminded me of a hurt and angry animal trying to lick its wounds with salt on its tongue."

"What made him change?"

"Time, I suppose," she offered.

"I wouldn't be so quick to give time *all* the credit."

She turned to him.

"Are you and he good friends?" he asked.

She sighed, "Yes, I would like to think so." Then Anna let out a little chuckle and added, "Oh, but if you could have seen us at the start! He didn't like me in the least, which was fine because I felt the same way about him. I think we could have easily despised each other for the rest of our lives. But after I discovered his wonderful talent for playing the piano, well, we've been doing lots of practicing together. Sometimes we talk a lot, and sometimes we let our instruments do the talking for us. I will never forget the first time I heard him playing a piece that I used to play on my violin. I used to dream that someone would accompany me on their piano while reading my mind."

The man suggested, "Wouldn't it be a lot easier if you wrote it down?"

She shook her head. "Can't. Don't know how."

"So you play by ear then?"

"Pretty much. When he played a piece that was swirling around in my brain for years, we kind of made a deal to help each other out. He needed me, and I needed him."

"Oh?" the man raised his eyebrows.

"No, nothing like that." She rubbed her hands together thoughtfully. "I needed his music and he wanted my company to keep him from being lonely out here. Of all people, he had to pick me, and I couldn't stand to be in the same church with him!"

He leaned forward on the counter. "And now?"

"I guess you could say that we've grown on each other, although, we had no intention of that ever happening . . ." Her voice trailed off.

He thought a minute before speaking, then chose his words carefully. "If you don't mind me saying so, I believe that a friendship such as yours could last a long time. It sounds like you've really taken the time to understand each other." He chuckled. "Some married folks live under the same roof, but they don't know each other anymore, and don't care. I guess for some people it's more convenient to stay and not care than it is to leave and be by yourself."

She took a sip of coffee. "So, you're running away from the Mrs.?"

The man let out a long sigh and shrugged his shoulders."

"I'm here for Thanksgiving. I'll head back on Friday or Saturday, or maybe tonight, depending on whether or not he wants to see me."

"Who's 'he?'"

"My son."

Anna hesitated, then asked, "Why wouldn't he want to see you?"

"Well, he's not really mad at me. It's his mother. A few weeks ago he called me and asked if he might invite a friend to Thanksgiving dinner. I said of course and was so looking forward to seeing my son. He lives such a long way from Seattle and we only talk to each other once or twice a month. Anyway, his mother gets on the phone and . . ." The man suddenly caught himself and closed his mouth quickly.

Anna couldn't stop herself. "And . . . what'd she say?" The words escaped her mouth almost before she noticed.

He shook his head and said, "I wanted to see my son, and I am going to see my son. We have a lot of catching up to do, *if* he'll let me."

"I feel sorry for your son, and for you."

"I think I feel more sorry for my wife." The stranger stared at the coffee machines in front of him. "Because she will never find out what a wonderful person my son has for a friend."

He put his coffee down, and slid off the stool, and as he began to reach for his wallet in his back pocket, Anna shook her head and said that his meal was on the house. He thanked her for the food and for the conversation, and wished her a wonderful Thanksgiving. As he put his coat back on, she got up from her stool and cleared away their coffee cups.

The man raised a hand wave to her, and she waved back. A bit of cold afternoon air came in the café door for a moment as the door shut behind him.

~*~

The dining room table was beautifully decorated with a white linen tablecloth and Anna's parents' wedding china, used only on Easter, Thanksgiving, and Christmas.

Anna placed the silverware chest on the raised hearth in front of the fire that glowed and crackled in the background. As she placed the elegant forks around the large table, she heard a popping sound in the fireplace. Going over to the brick hearth, she grabbed a handful of knives from the maroon felt lining of the dark cherry silverware chest. After the chest was emptied, she sat by the fire, warmed her back, and gently closed the lid on the wedding present from long ago. Anna wondered if she would ever be able to receive such gifts, and be able to put them out each year on a fine table with a blazing fire in the hearth in her *own* home.

She admired the floral centerpiece made up of yellow, orange, and white chrysanthemums, several large white carnations, greenery, berry branches, and two graceful, tapered orange candles. Flanking the centerpiece were two ceramic turkeys facing the ends of the table. One turkey would be staring at her father and the other at her mother. Every Easter, every Thanksgiving, and every Christmas, the family sat in the same place, year after year. No one ever disputed the seating arrangement. And soon, Pastor Edwards would be joining them. Most likely, he would be sitting next to her father, and she would sit next to him.

Anna's thoughts brought her back to the day before, and she wondered about the stranger and how he was getting along with his son. She hoped that they would be going somewhere today, and then wished that she had invited him to her parents' house, just in case things didn't go well. The thought of him driving all the way back to Seattle on Thanksgiving Day made her heart ache for the poor man.

The phone in the living room rang and someone picked it up.

"Mom, it's for you!"

Mrs. McManus, clattering around in the kitchen, called over her shoulder, "I'm kind of busy right now. Find out who it is and tell them I'll call them back."

"It's Pastor Edwards. He wants to ask you something," returned the voice.

"Oh! I'm coming . . ." A lid clattered onto a pot just before she emerged from the kitchen door, wiping her hands on a kitchen towel.

On her way through the dining room to the living room, Mrs. McManus told Anna that there was a pot of potatoes that needed mashing after she put the silverware chest away. Anna got up from the hearth and leaned against the corner of the wall leading into the living room. Her mother was speaking to James on the phone, which was rare. Maybe, she thought, he couldn't make it for some reason and wanted to apologize to her mother instead. There was head-nodding, a "yes," an "I see," a series of "uh-huhs," followed by a cheerful "by all means!" She put the phone down and headed back to the kitchen with Anna following her.

"Well?"

"Well, what?"

"What did James want? Is he still coming?"

"Yes, Anna, he is coming. Can you please get those potatoes mashed or else when he does get here, there won't be any."

"But Mom, why did he want to talk to you, and not to me?"

Mrs. McManus turned to her daughter, and put a hand on her hip.

"Pastor Edwards was asking *me* a question. Now get mashing those potatoes. I have something that needs to be done in the other room."

Mrs. McManus, her three younger daughters, and Anna were carrying bowls of black olives, watermelon-rind pickles, cucumber rings, pickled beets, cranberry sauce, raspberry-apple conserve, potato rolls, and butter to the table when there was a knock at the front door.

Anna heard her father greet Pastor Edwards, and the voices of her three brothers mixed in. She would have poked her head into the other room, but there were things that still needed to be done in the warm and busy kitchen. Salads, stuffing, and the bowl of mashed potatoes passed her by as she entered the kitchen. Her mother gave her two bowls of gravy, and as she stood next to the table, two of her sisters came out with steaming bowls of beans and kernel corn. The three of them looked at the swelling table and then at each other, and burst out laughing at the wonderful but full table before them.

"And *where* are we supposed to put these?" one

of the sisters asked.

Putting the two bowls of gravy down on two plates, Anna did a little rearranging and some squeezing, made room for the vegetables, and prayed that that was it.

One of the girls spoke up. "I hope that Dad never expects *me* to work in that café of yours when I get out of high school. Ugh! I would *hate* to do this for a living!"

Anna looked at her fourteen-year-old sister and shot back, "Oh, God forbid! You just better hope and pray that you can get plenty of scholarships like Gareth did, so you won't have to stand on your feet for ten to twelve hours a day. God forbid that your sister is helping out the family and helping put Gareth through college. You just better hope and pray that you do well in school so you can get a decent job. What a shame it would be to waste your life in such a lowly, unrewarding profession. Oh, did I say profession? *Excuse* me. I should have known better than to use the words *waitressing* and *profession* in the same breath. God forbid you should ever end up like *me!*"

The two sisters looked at each other, and the twelve-year-old asked, "Well then, why don't you do something *else* if you don't like what you do? That's what I'd do. I'm going far away from here and marry someone rich. I want to see tall buildings, not combines going back and forth, back and forth all day long. And I want to walk through busy streets filled with people in business suits instead of walking through endless, endless fields of wheat."

"Amen to *that!*" the fourteen-year-old agreed.

Anna confronted the pair of them. "Who *says* I

don't like what I do?"

"Didn't you just say what a lousy life waitressing is?"

"No, you did."

"Jeez Anna, you're getting too weird! But, oh well, as long as you want to do the dirty work and put us through college so we can get out of this place and marry someone as handsome as Pastor Edwards, well—you can be as weird as you want."

Mrs. McManus was calling the girls to come back into the kitchen, and while Anna turned to face the fireplace, the two sisters laughed and left her alone staring into the flames. Anna did not feel like sitting down at the big table to take part in the wonderful things that she and her mother made from their garden over the summer. Her two sisters had put a damper on her mood and made her feel as if what she did every day was a worthless job compared to their young, carefree lives. Although they were much younger, their ungratefulness towards their parents and towards her was inexcusable. Anna wanted to go up to her room and be alone, and just as she was making her way up the steps a voice stopped her.

"Anna—there you are. Come back down, there's someone I want you to meet."

Slowly turning around, she saw James waiting for her at the bottom of the stairwell.

"Happy Thanksgiving!" he greeted her as he came up the stairs.

"Yeah." She let the word hang on the air.

James looked down at her, sympathetically, put his hands on her shoulders, and asked if anything was wrong. There wasn't much she could say except that she wished she were in her room away from everyone else. And if she couldn't retreat to her room, she would have to suffer the constant chatter of voices—except for hers, then everyone would wonder what was the matter with her. So Anna shook her head and let James take her hand and lead her into the family room.

His back was facing her as he spoke to Mr. McManus, but it was his overcoat with the sheepskin collar that gave him away. Her father stopped talking and looked at Pastor Edwards and Anna. Turning around, the stranger stood before her with the same gentle grin that he had worn just the day before. James was still holding her hand when he looked at her and said, "Anna, I'd like you to meet my dad, Charles Edwards."

Anna looked at the man, and then at his son, and then saw the resemblance. In his youth he must have looked a lot like James, and she wondered what James' mom looked like. She had heard that sons were often attracted to women who look like their mothers. Anna carefully looked into the eyes of the stranger and regarded him as such, for she had told him many things concerning the other man beside her. Had she known who he was, she would not have spoken so freely to him.

Anna was aware of many eyes falling on her, and Mr. Edwards' gentle grin had not completely disappeared.

James' dad's voice was soft when he asked Anna if anything was wrong.

"That all depends, Mr. Edwards." Anna crossed her

arms under her chest.

"Anna? Dad?" James looked at both of them, but they ignored him.

"You were a stranger yesterday," murmured Anna. "Today you are not—completely."

The gentle smile returned. "I was," he acknowledged.

"We spoke of many *things* yesterday."

"We did," he agreed.

Anna lifted her eyebrows and the man's face softened and his grin grew.

"You and I cannot be all that different, Mr. Edwards," she remarked. "I believe that there are many things in life that are spoken and shared, while other things must be kept to oneself."

He nodded. "I agree. To do otherwise, dear friend of my only son, would be a foolish thing to do, since I highly value the words from yesterday, more than you'll ever know."

"Good. You are welcome to stay. Let me take your coat, Charles, for I believe dinner is ready and the mashed potatoes are getting cold."

Anna led Mr. Edwards into the dining room with a pastor and father in tow. James bent his head towards Mr. McManus.

"What was all that about?"

He shrugged his shoulders, and then at the same time both men said, "With Anna, who knows?"

Family, friends, and fathers took a seat at the crowded table. With heads bowed in prayer, Richard McManus asked that his family be blessed with continued health and happiness. He thanked God for a good year in the fields, and then gave a special thanks to his eldest daughter for managing the café. Now that Mother Earth was resting for the winter, it was Anna's hard work and long hours that would help support them through the long, cold months ahead.

If Anna had looked up, she would have noticed a stark realization covering her younger sisters' faces when their father was blessing Anna. Had the words *not* come from *his* mouth, the sincerity and importance would have been meaningless to them. Unknown to him, his words slapped their faces and stung.

Directly after a noisy amen, the turkey was rolled out on a serving cart and placed next to Mr. McManus. The first two servings were given to the guests, and then around the table bowls of this and that were emptied. Mrs. McManus urged James and his father to try the homemade relishes that Anna made.

"With your help," Anna added. "Thank you, Mom."

James grinned at Anna while she tried not to look embarrassed from her mother's intentional prodding which was meant for him. He looked over at Mr. McManus who was making small talk with his dad in-between bites, and his dad, who was never one to make conversation with strangers, was actually talking between nodding and eating.

He slowed down and looked around him at the large family, the large table, and people talking but not being able to understand any particular conversation. They were all rolled into one. James found himself resting an elbow on the edge of the table with his fork suspended between his fingers. He couldn't help but take it all in. He knew this family wasn't perfect. They had their share of issues just like any other family. Each sibling probably couldn't stand one of his or her brothers or sisters. But here they were, together.

His eyes found a wedge between two bodies, and while staring at the fire, James remembered many family Thanksgivings where only three people were there to celebrate it.

The only time James had looked forward to the holidays was when his dad's brother and wife came over from the other side of the mountains. These occasions occurred only every other year or so. When he was in his teens, James realized that his uncle and aunt probably would have visited more often, but his mother's effect on people couldn't be ignored. His aunt, the more gracious one, kept her mouth shut. Their visits were always cut short, the years in-between visits lengthened, and soon they stopped coming altogether. James moved his stare to his dad, and wondered why in the hell he put up with such crap. Why did he take such abuse from a dysfunctional, warped, domineering wife?

It took a split second to happen—a sharp clattering sound halted voices and mouths, heads jerking toward the noise. He first felt all eyes upon him, and then a horrible, heavy silence quickly rushed in and pushed against his chest. His eyes did not want to move.

"You dropped your fork," Anna whispered. "I'll get you another." She smiled and tried to push her chair out.

"No, I will."

"But you don't know where—"

"I'll find it!"

His voice was not spoken in whispers. Nor was it

soft. His words were firm and few, and it was the first time anyone had ever witnessed their pastor with moist eyes. He was not gentle in removing himself from his cramped enclosure, for his own emotions escalated at the rising fear that he, their own pastor, would be caught weeping.

After James hastily retreated for the kitchen, the occupants around the table sat rigid, afraid to utter the first word. Anna got up and picked up the chair that lay on its back. She began to walk toward the kitchen door but was stopped by Mr. Edwards.

"I'll go to him. He's my son," he calmly announced.

James' father stood up, neatly folded his napkin and placed it to the right of his plate. He apologized for James, saying that his son was probably just feeling overwhelmed. He asked that everyone please continue enjoying the wonderful meal, and that he and James would be back shortly.

Entering the kitchen as quietly as he could, he saw his son leaning against the kitchen window sink crying. His shoulders were slouched forward and his upper body shook. The father let out a heavy sigh and placed a hand on his son's trembling shoulder. In a low, angry voice, James finally spit out the words, "I hate her Dad—I just *hate* her!"

James filled his lungs with the air that was still laden with the aroma from the feast that awaited them in the other room, and turning around to hug his father, his breath left him in violent sobs. It was the first time since he was a little boy that he cried on his dad's shoulder.

"I know son. I know."

James composed himself, and he and his dad sat down.

The father gathered his thoughts, and then looked across the table at his son.

"I'm leaving your mother."

James could only sit in shock at the prospect of what this meant for his father.

"James, I can't tell you how sorry I am about what your mother said to you on the phone."

"Dad, don't refer to her as my mother." James shook his head. "Please, never again. That *person* said that Anna was *not* welcome in *her* home because she does not have a *desirable* job, because she is a *farmer's* daughter and isn't a social climber. Therefore, she did not want to meet Anna."

Mr. Edwards bowed his head and sighed.

"That's too bad, because she will never know that young lady out there." He paused. "They don't make 'em like that anymore."

"That's for sure!" said James decisively. "By the way, what was that little thing earlier with you and Anna? She said that you two *talked*."

"We did, at the café."

"And you're not going to tell me anything about it, are you?"

"Correct."

"That's all right, I probably already know. Don't I?"

"Probably."

The kitchen was quiet, but it was a nice kind of quiet as the two men sat staring at the table.

"So what are you going to do now?" James ventured.

"Well, since I still have another five or six years left until I retire, I suppose I'll find an apartment close to work, and figure things out one day at a time."

"You can always stay with me," James offered, "I would love to have you. I mean it."

The father smiled at his son.

"I just might take you up on that offer, but just on the weekends. I wouldn't want to interfere with you and Anna."

"She's something else, isn't she?"

"James, I have never told you once how to live your life. Have I?"

"No, not that I can recall."

"Good, then this will be the first and the last time. Don't let Anna get away. But, if you do let her go," the father paused long enough to hold his son's attention, "*that*, will be the only and biggest mistake you will have ever made."

"But what if she doesn't want me? What if she doesn't want to be the wife of a pastor?" he asked in a worried voice.

"James, you know as well as I do, that Anna is nothing like . . ." he hesitated. "I'm sorry if she hurt you, but I can thank God that she turned you down. If there's anybody on this earth that I would *love* to have for a daughter-in-law, it's that young lady out there."

"You think so, huh?"

"Yep."

The humming of low voices in the next room trickled into the kitchen. The two men looked at each other, and both knew that things were going to be okay. The elder Edwards began to rise from his seat, but James said that he wanted to ask him something.

"Who did she hate first? You or me?"

The father sat down and stared at his son. "What kind of a question is that?"

James explained, "A long time ago, when I was a kid, I asked her one day why I didn't have a brother or sister. She laughed at me and said that she hated being pregnant with me. That the ugliness of a swelling belly and the torment of a body splitting in two should be reserved for cats and dogs who didn't know any better. She said she never wanted children in the first place, but you would have divorced her if she didn't at least have one baby, even if she didn't want it. It was the only time that you got your way, she said, and after that, she made sure that you never did again."

His father's head was bent and he was looking down at his folded hands. Then he looked up and said firmly, "Except for your piano lessons. I made darn sure that she wasn't going to interfere with those."

James smiled wryly. "Thanks, Dad."

"You're welcome, son."

"Dad, have I ever told you that I love you?"

Mr. Edwards stretched, leaning back in his chair, smiling affectionately at his son. "Well, perhaps never in words, but I've always known in my heart." With that, he stood up. "And *now*, if you're done talking, I would like to go back to the dining room and finish my dinner."

As they left the kitchen, James advised his father, "Save some room for Anna's rum cake. I understand that the sauce will throw you for a loop."

Mr. Edwards clapped a hand down on James's shoulder. "Good! I believe that's *just* what we need."

## CHAPTER 11—THE LAMP LIGHTER

The copper-colored clock on the kitchen wall said it was half past five in the evening on the first Tuesday of January. Snowflakes had been drifting down from the heavens ever since breakfast and brightened the world around his snug little house.

Just two days before, after the Sunday service was over, James was treated to a surprise party in his honor to celebrate his one-year anniversary as pastor of the little white church. The old calendar lay on the counter, not far from the new one that had photos of country churches during the four seasons. It was a gift from Mr. and Mrs. Krumbly—one of many gifts presented to him at the party.

Although James was not a sentimental fool by nature, he could not imagine throwing the old calendar away, as each square of every month held some sort of memory for him. Almost from the beginning he had found himself writing little notes down every day, and more often than not, such events became the cornerstone of a sermon or a joke which became a way of connecting with his flock.

There was the time when a toilet greeted him on someone's front lawn. The culprit was a runaway cloth diaper.

Another memorable time was when he made an unannounced visit to a woman in her early eighties the previous summer. After much knocking on the front door, James made his way to the backyard where he thought he might find her sipping lemonade and would be offered one too. Instead, he was offered a lot more than a glass of refreshment on that hot summer day. For among the flowers for which she was tenderly weeding, he found her in the buff, completely naked except for an elaborate straw sun hat.

He learned how to operate combines, helped turn a calf around inside its mother, and deliver the damp-haired, wide-eyed little creature that was later named after him. The farmers put soil in his smooth hands and told him a thing or two about planting crops, both the risks and the rewards of it all.

Anna had been right in making him go at it alone in getting to know the community.

Each Sunday when he faced the congregation, he wasn't just seeing and speaking to faces. The folks who came through the double doors were his friends, and James felt a special bond with each of them.

A smile lingered on his face, for it was not so long ago that his heart ached because of another Eve; wherever she was. James felt good that he could smile at himself. He savored the happiness of the moment, for his heart did not ache for the city on the other side of the mountains. Last January seemed a long, long time ago.

Leaning against the kitchen counter with his arms crossed under his chest, James stared at the kitchen around him and let out a healthy sigh. The kitchen evoked deep memories of that April morning before he and Anna had made their friendship pact.

Before that, there was his first day in town when he met Anna, and Curly too. He thought about Mrs. Krumbly, his first sermon, Anna's abrupt departure, and the dead fly.

Then there was February and March that came and went without Anna's presence among the congregation. A visit from her younger brother Gareth prompted James to make a mandatory visit to her parent's home.

It wasn't until early April when Anna paid *him* an early morning visit that both of them declared a truce. From that day on she never missed a Sunday service in the little white church.

May had come, painting the fields in yellows and shades of green, and then there was that wonderful evening in June when Anna drank the blush wine on his front porch steps. July and August gave summer a new meaning to the former city dweller who was not accustomed to the hot, dry weather. They were also the months where the fields turned brown and gold.

But of all the months thus far, September had to have been the best. What a night. It was the first time he had held Anna and danced with her. After that night under the harvest moon, his relationship with her grew stronger and deeper.

It was the night that he wanted her all to himself. And it was during that wonderful evening that he knew he wanted Anna McManus.

James knew that in his life there were only a handful of memories that were so completely clear they would never fade away. One was that he was still able to feel Anna; his arms closely wrapped around her as they stood under the bright harvest moon sky. The other memory was on that same night, as he could have sworn he heard the breeze whispering to the orchard trees.

James went over to the kitchen table and peered outside the window. The wind howled against the window frame, and he noticed that the snowflakes were growing larger. James loved the way the snow spread a perfect, fluffy blanket over the quiet landscape.

Close to the back of the house was a woodpile covered with a tarp topped with snow. Before a Sunday afternoon dinner in early autumn at the McManus house, James saw something he had never seen before. From their kitchen window he saw Anna swinging an ax and splitting wood. He had asked her father why one of the boys weren't out there instead.

Anna's father had grinned at James.

"That's *her* job."

Still not understanding what he meant, James asked again, "You mean she *has* to do that?"

Mr. McManus shook his head. "You don't understand. Anna won't *let* us do it. She wants to do it. She loves the sound of the cracking wood. She loves how it makes her strong. You couldn't take that ax away from her if you tried, so don't even ask."

But James did, and she showed him how to split

wood without chopping his legs off. And so the pile of wood that proudly sat in his backyard was of his own making.

Alone with his thoughts, James went to the front door and turned on the porch light, as winter's evening darkness had already set in. His eyes danced as they tried to follow the crystal flakes while they blew across the path of light. They were beautiful, but his thoughts were on Anna and where she might be. Although there was no doubt in his mind that Anna could handle driving through a snowstorm, things could happen—even to the best of drivers.

He went back into the kitchen and called the café. No answer. He waited a moment or two and then called the McManus household. One of her younger sisters said that Anna had called them a bit ago and was just locking up for the night. James was glad to hear that she was closing early, but undoubtedly, that meant she was heading straight home. What he didn't expect to hear from her sister was that Anna was planning to stop at his place briefly with soup or something—but just briefly.

The sister had cleared her throat and concluded the conversation with, "She *is* expected home."

He slowly hung up the phone and sighed, before saying to no one in particular, "Imagine that. She *is* expected home."

James thought about putting the percolator on which he had mastered long ago, but instead, he turned on a burner and poured apple cider into a kettle. Finding some cinnamon sticks in the pantry, he added them to the kettle. He got out two nice cups and saucers, and then James thought of one more thing back in the pantry.

His ears heard a familiar sound and quickly made his way to the front door to see a pair of headlights dimming. Meeting Anna on the steps, James took a small covered pot from her and turned back to the porch.

"I'm glad you made it. I was getting worried."

"Aw, this is nothin'," she remarked, shaking snow off her hood.

"I thought you might say something like that."

"Oh, did you? What else do you know?"

"I know that I probably should thank you for whatever you brought me, turn you back to your truck, and tell you to go straight home. You *are* expected there."

Anna lifted her face, sniffed the air, and searched the air with her eyes as if they could see some pleasing aroma wafting about. She went up the steps and in the house before he could stop her.

"What are you doing?"

Anna had started peeling off layers of outerwear, flinging them onto the arm of the sofa.

"I'm going to sit down and enjoy a cup of hot apple cider," she announced, almost defiantly.

She sniffed the aroma again, then added, "There's something missin'. Ah! I know! You forgot the whole cloves."

James shifted his feet uneasily. "Listen Anna, maybe you ought to go . . . just so your folks don't worry."

Anna headed toward the kitchen. "Nope, don't

think so. I've just spent the last thirty minutes in a truck that doesn't have much of a heater and I'm not going to run home just because I'm *expected* there. While I call my folks to let them know I made it here, you pour the cider, and then I'll heat us up some beef barley soup." She disappeared into the kitchen as she spoke.

Without realizing it, James stood there grinning. Quietly he sang, "*Let it snow, let it snow, let it snow . . .*"

A while later, James and Anna sat full and contented as the light from the kerosene lamp seemed to warm the kitchen's atmosphere, glowing softly into every corner.

They looked out the window when a gust of wind pushed against it, but they didn't say anything. James gently knocked on the thin glass and made a quiet comment about getting thermal pane windows before next winter.

Anna nodded toward the potbelly woodstove that was heating the room and commented on how nice and cozy the kitchen was because of it. Squeezing his upper arm, she reminded him that he didn't split a cord of wood for nothing. James made a casual comment concerning the depth of snow beyond their walls, and Anna's response was that her warm, full stomach would feel more comfortable on the sofa.

Although the living room lights were in working order, it was the warm glow from the kerosene lamp that lit the room and bathed those near it in tranquility. During much conversation that steered clear of any mention of company departing, Anna covered a yawn and said it had been a long and tiring day. James found and extra blanket and covered Anna while she stretched out on the sofa and rested her head on a pillow.

Settling back into his favorite chair, he asked her to tell him the story about the area's longest power outage. She yawned a full yawn and thought a moment, and then yawned again, finishing with a small, sleepy grin. Then she began:

"It was the winter the grape arbor fell down. Ivory flakes poured from heaven. Schoolyards missed their children and their laughter. Snow paraphernalia was resurrected. I forget what year it was exactly. It was the winter we held shovels in our hands, digging out the driveway for dad. There's six of us kids—half were too young to help in the knee-deep stuff. Mom promised us hot chocolate with miniature marshmallows, a soothing warm bath to thaw our bodies. Half frozen, mom ended up sick; we took care of her.

Dad made it to work, though I don't know how. I'm sure he tried out of necessity; first to feed eight mouths, and second, sparing himself from spending a day cooped up with us as dads are not accustomed to such things.

It was the year the power was out for a week. We convened to the kitchen, and to the family room, which was heated by the monarch stove. We nearly suffocated from the heat.

I made several trips to the coal bin. In the blackness against the soft blanket of snow an animal ran in front of my feet, dragging a long tail. I clenched the pail and shovel. I gulped and got my coal.

Family unity was put to the test as well as the endurance of my parent's sanity. We managed to get along. Conversation actually replaced television. A sense of family was very real in those two rooms for a week. Power was restored, but the grape arbor was laid to rest."

Anna yawned again as she finished her narrative, and James yawned too.

The kettle of apple cider was still on the stove, and he could not remember if it was turned off. When he returned, the occupant on the couch was looking peaceful and was sound asleep. James covered her with another blanket, tucked it in around her neck, and made a phone call to the McManus household.

The wick was turned down and blown out with one puff.

While the rest of the world was covered in a blanket of white, no one saw James bend down to kiss her head and stroke her hair before he wished her goodnight. He found himself wanting to be near Anna, even if it meant just watching her sleep. It was a ridiculous idea, so he made himself go to his room.

But lying in bed and closing one's eyes does not guarantee sleep, especially when a man's mind is not at rest. A long hour passed, which found James pacing in front of the chilly window with his arms tightly crossed in front of him.

Now and then he stared out the window to watch the wind push the snow into waving drifts, and occasionally the wind kicked up a handful of crystals in front of his face, where they stuck to the cold glass. As he studied the snow on the thin window, a soft yellow glow illuminated it. The source of the comforting light came from his open door.

"James," Anna whispered, "I cannot sleep. It's too

quiet out there."

"And it is—or was, too dark in here."

"May I stay and warm myself under the feathers?" Anna hugged herself with her arms and shivered.

James folded back the thick goose down comforter and patted the mattress. Anna came into the room and set the lamp on the nightstand beside the bed, then crawled under the covers.

"Better?" he asked while covering himself with the thick, downy feathers.

She nodded.

James gathered that perhaps as much as Anna liked her moments of solitude, she was not exposed to it often at her house. The woman next to him would not look his way, for although her footsteps were courageous in carrying her this far, perhaps the apprehension of the unfamiliar could only summon timidness.

"I think I would like to hear another one of your stories. If you have another, that is." he prompted.

"I just might."

She drew her knees closer to her body, hugged them, and began.

"Once upon a time, there were two people, a man and a woman. In the summer, they lay under the heavens watching meteor showers and explained constellations to each other. In the autumn, they jumped in pyramids of maple and oak leaves. And, with the man's help, they carved dozens of pumpkins for a Harvest Dance."

"Don't remind me!" James grumbled at the memory with a grin.

She continued, "In the winter, they made angels in

virgin snow, and made a snowman and a snowwoman . . ."

Anna dropped her eyes.

"I'm not saying what I want to say." She sighed, glanced away and pulled the covers closer to her. She ventured, "I know we made a promise, a long time ago. . ."

The room was silent and still, and the walls strained to listen, and her lips whispered words that James only dreamt of.

"I want to break that promise tonight."

James turned to his side, facing her. He knew Anna only said things she was sure of, so he didn't bother asking out loud. Instead, he raised his eyebrows and she read his mind. Anna lay her head down on the pillow.

"Wasn't it *I* who lit the lamp, and brought it to *you*?" He softly kissed her forehead, and then her lips. "Anything else, Miss Anna?" he whispered.

"Can we stop talking?" she whispered back.

"That won't be a prob—" His lips were silenced. Beyond the softly lit walls, swirls of crystalline dancers knocked on the thin windows in hopes of an audience. But tonight, there would be none.

## CHAPTER 12—THE FIELD OF STONES

The afternoon sun in mid-May was a wonderful thing to experience while sitting on his porch step, lighting and puffing on a pipe that he took up last autumn, blissfully enjoying the black-cherry tobacco aroma. His arms were warm and his face turned in the direction that the warmth came from.

Spring surrounded James with lush grass, soft and brilliantly-colored flowers, and the sounds of bees inside the hearts of tulips.

For a moment he closed his eyes and life was wonderful. Birds were singing beyond the house and he took another puff on his pipe. But a new sound interrupted the song that the birds were singing. A car was making its way up the driveway, and as it got closer, he recognized the woman behind the wheel and groaned. James removed the pipe from his mouth and breathed deeply. His stomach felt hard as if a rock had just hit bottom.

The car came to rest in a small swirl of dust, and in the dust two plump feet in tight shoes were planted.

"Pastor Edwards . . . it looks like you are enjoying a bit of 'our' spring once again," she beamed at him.

Briefly making eye contact with Mrs. Barker, he dismissed her and gazed at his flowers.

"I am," he finally replied.

She cleared her throat and folded her hands in front of her ample mid-section, then spoke.

"I was planning to call you later, but as I was nearing your house, I thought I saw you on the porch and wondered if I might speak to you now. I will just take a moment of your time."

James eyed the woman and slowly placed his pipe between his teeth and puffed.

"Only for a moment or two," he agreed cautiously.

Mrs. Barker could not hide the look of displeasure that spread over her features.

She raised an eyebrow in his direction before suggesting, "Perhaps we could go inside where it's more comfortable?"

"Inside?" James shook his head, smiling in apparent disbelief. "When God gives us a beautiful day such as today, we shouldn't waste it under a roof."

Mrs. Barker eyed the steps for dust particles, and then carefully settled herself down on the same step but at a healthy distance from the young pastor.

James enjoyed watching her, as she was out of her element of usual habitat. She sat nervously toying with her wedding ring; turning the cluster of diamonds as to make them dance on her finger. He pretended not to notice and smoked his pipe, breathing in the air about him.

While she was in the middle of picking invisible lint off her slacks, James asked, "Was there something that you wanted to speak to me about?" James looked straight at the woman and raised his eyebrows with a bored look.

"Well, yes of course," she replied, delicately flicking the lint off her fingertips.

Mrs. Barker carefully prepared her voice. "It has come to my attention that you were seen at a jewelry store recently."

James continued to smoke his pipe and glance out at the flowers basking in the warmth of the day. When Mrs. Barker got the hint that there would be no reply, a blanket of tension was draped over the two. But this did not bother James, for in an odd way he was rather enjoying himself.

"Pastor Edwards," Mrs. Barker readjusted her position on the steps and tried again. "Although you and I haven't been, well, good friends in the past, if we could just put our personalities aside, you would see that in the long run, my daughter would make a suitable wife for you." Mrs. Barker leaned forward slightly to gauge his reaction.

James continued to smoke his pipe and fill the air with the black-cherry tobacco. He did not glance at the woman on his left.

Mrs. Barker was undeterred. "There probably isn't another woman more *eligible* to be a pastor's wife. She is an exceptional cook, a wonderful housekeeper, and knows her Bible forwards and backwards. She could help you in so *many* ways!" Her words tumbled out in a rush.

"She sounds suitable enough," James conceded. "But—is she in *love* with me?" James turned his head and looked at the woman who was looking elsewhere. "Mrs. Barker, does your daughter *love* me?" he repeated.

The woman next to him did not respond well to his questioning. She nervously twitched and wanted to pace like a caged animal being watched.

The question was asked a third time. "Does she love me? Could she ever love me?"

"I don't know . . . but love is *irrelevant* here!" she sputtered, her irritation growing to rage.

"Irrelevant!?" A hearty laugh was thrown into the air. "For whom? Marriage means *nothing* if there isn't love between a man and a woman. It's the glue which holds a husband and wife together. I feel sorry for your daughter if she hasn't been able to learn the meaning of love because you find it *irrelevant*. As far as your daughter goes, she is probably capable of finding a husband on her own, *if* that's what she wants, without your involvement."

Mrs. Barker suddenly found her voice. "I don't have to listen to this!" she spat, quickly rising from the steps and storming off toward her car.

James' voice followed her down the drive. "I am curious though, why you have a difficult time with the theory of love. Tell me this. Have you ever really loved anyone?"

Mrs. Barker stopped and spun around to face Pastor Edwards. Her face was hard and chilled, and a river of cold water ran down his spine, for the woman who stood before him appeared as if she had been prepared for viewing in a funeral parlor. She walked back to him and got right up to his face.

"A mother cannot love after her heart has been ripped from her body. You see, my dear *former* pastor," she seethed, "it was *my* son who was killed by the person whom you think you are in love with." She tightened her hands into a fist. "My son is *gone* and my heart is buried with him. Does that answer your question, Pastor Edwards?"

She turned away from him, but remembering something else, she craned her head around.

"Never, *ever*, underestimate the wrath of a mother. Especially, the mother of a dead son."

Her words were repeated again and again inside his head until memory found what it was searching for. It was the night under the harvest moon that Anna had told him, "I underestimated someone and I paid the price."

Standing in front of him was the person who hurt the one he loved. The flow of rage that ran through his body was poisonous, and he was afraid of himself because he could actually taste the venom.

"Leave this property at *once*!" he hissed.

"What's the matter, Pastor Edwards?" The plump woman turned herself around to face him. "She didn't tell you about my son, did she? I didn't think so. Well, your perfect day is about to turn ugly."

"Leave now before I do something I might not regret!"

She planted her plump feet and placed her hands on her hips. "Are you *threatening* me?" she blustered.

"Do you want to find out?"

"I could bring you down for such harassment!"

James drenched his laugh with ridicule. "Do

yourself a favor and get yourself a life, and leave your poor daughter out of it!"

Mrs. Barker got in her car and slammed the door. She looked at James, and her smile was smeared with the devil's paintbrush.

"Let her tell you about my dead son. You will find them in the field of stones." Her eyes gleamed. "And after today, she won't have been the *only* fool to have underestimated me!"

The dust had settled back on the earth while her car was not quite out of sight, but James could only stand there. His mind was not functioning, so his body took over and led him back into the house. His fingers picked up the keys to his truck and let the front door half close behind him.

His truck seemed to do the driving, for his mind was dull and slow to respond. The air that ran over his arm and onto his chest felt cool. The truck slowed down and made a right-hand turn into the entrance of the cemetery. It came to a stop and the engine was turned off.

James saw one lone figure sitting in the field of stones.

He sat in his truck watching her back, and his mind and body felt as if he had had one too many beers. Bewilderment staggered over his numbness, but this did not stop his left hand from opening the door or stop his legs from getting out of the truck. A part of him wanted to hesitate forever, but fear is also curious and it led him slowly forward.

The warm afternoon sun was at his back, and it cast a shadow before him. The man and his shadow slowed down and came to a stop behind her, and the shadow partially fell upon the young woman who sat with her legs crossed.

She turned her head slightly to the left as if she were looking at the shadow and said, "Hello, James."

"Hello, Anna."

"If you intend to join me, please move your shadow or sit down beside me."

As he settled himself upon the earth, he glanced over at Anna. She had her eyes closed and he sensed that she would be with him when she was ready.

On that May afternoon, over farmland and prairie grass, a slight breeze came in waves. It brushed against them and a little smile appeared on her face.

"Are your eyes closed, James?"

He nodded out of habit and replied with a quiet, "Yes."

"Today, I needed to be caressed by the breeze, touched by the wind, and held by the warmth of the sun. And now, it is time for you to know *why* I am here."

Fear grabbed a hold of him again, and he wanted to prolong the truth, but a voice inside him spoke without his permission.

"Mrs. Barker stopped by the house."

Anna replied tranquilly, "Yes, I thought she might. It was just a matter of time before she would. What did she tell you?"

"That she had a son, and that you are to blame for his death."

Anna stood up and offered him a hand. "Come with me."

They walked on for a short distance, James

following a few steps behind Anna. She stood in front of a row of stones and folded her arms under her chest, but she did not point or look down at any one in particular.

"Which one?" James quietly asked.

Anna held her head up and took a deep breath from the air around her. "Finnegan. David Finnegan."

James looked down to his left and saw the dark marble stone with the name on it. He slowly let himself down and rested himself on his heels.

"In case you're wondering, he was from Mrs. Barker's first husband."

"Only 23?"

"Only 23. I was almost 20."

"Anna, what happened?"

She was silent and he looked up at her while she was having difficulty swallowing, but her eyes still did not look down. "David was drunk when he was driving home from his bachelor party. He drove into a telephone pole and died."

"Oh God!"

"I can't tell you what it was like hearing my mother on the phone telling every 'would have been' guest that there would be no wedding. I can't tell you how I pleaded with David to not drive if he drank. He promised he wouldn't."

James stood next to her and let out a heavy sigh.

"And ever since that night, for the past seven years, David's mother has hated my guts."

James was astounded. "But it wasn't your fault. So why does she hate you so much?"

Anna turned to look at him. "My fault was that I

loved her only son. If it wasn't me, it would have been someone else destined for her wrath."

"Anna," he said slowly, "she told me something I don't understand."

"What was that?"

"To never underestimate her."

Anna turned to James. "Don't."

"*What* does that mean?" he asked with a touch of impatience.

"Let me show you."

They turned and headed back towards his truck in the area where he first found her, and there, Anna paused. Kneeling beside a gray granite grave marker etched in leaves, vines and birds, Anna ran her fingers over the name "Baby McManus."

After James lowered himself down beside her, he knew that she knew his unspoken thoughts.

"This was not David's child. A few months after he died, I was beaten and raped one night after work. While my attacker was beating me, he kept saying, 'Never underestimate the mother of a dead son.'"

James bowed his head and pressed his eyes closed, struggling mentally to cease words and actions meant for Mrs. Barker, and knowing that his Heavenly Father knew his every thought did not help. "Oh Anna, I'm so sorry!" he whispered under his breath.

Anna pushed a few pieces of grass back from the stone. "Nine months later I brought a little girl into this world, but she only lived for 3 hours."

Anna's voice was beginning to shake and she wiped her eyes with the back of her hand.

"I—I didn't give her a name. I wasn't given time

to be with her. I would have had—a daughter who's seven. But she was taken away from me. She was taken away from me!"

Anna fell into James' arms and cried, and he cried for his past lack of sensitivity. They held onto each other until Anna broke the silence between them.

"Before my father was born, his parents lost their oldest son, little LeRoy who died of scarlet fever in 1931. He was only three years old. I don't know how a mother and father go on with their lives after they lose a child."

"One summer vacation
We drove and drove
to where dad
once was a boy
Osnabrook Township
6 miles from Fairdale
Grandpa Bob was part
of the soil named
North Dakota
He was born there
On a visit
with his wife
he died there

A blond-haired boy
squinted in the sun
his picture taken
on his trike
God bless him

An uncle I would have had
but little LeRoy
walked home
with pretty angels

We drove and drove
to where dad was born
The poor house was battered
and bruised by the elements
A city holds no horizons
but the warm wind brushed
the prairie grass to the end
where the striking blue sky
and puffy clouds
embraced and laughed
I wished I could have
known his thoughts
shared his sorrows
as dad stood on the prairie.

For a few moments
time was his;
we were not there
We drove and drove
back to where
we came from."

## CHAPTER 13—THE VELVET BOX

It was well past seven in the evening when James flopped his tired fingers on his lap. "No more." He pleaded with Anna. "No more!"

Anna grinned. "Ah, come on! It's only been an hour and a half. I'm just getting warmed up." She plucked a ringing note on one of the violin strings for emphasis.

"Anna, you wore me out. There isn't any feeling left in my fingers." James tried to hold them up from his lap and wiggle them. "See?"

Holding her violin in one hand and the bow in the other, she dropped her arms in protest. "Party pooper!" she huffed in protest while suppressing a smile.

"That's me." James leaned his head against the fallboard that the music sheet rested on and yawned. Anna bent down and kissed him softly on the lips and smiled.

"You did pretty good tonight." James said after

kissing her in return.

"And you aren't too bad yourself," Anna teased.

"Gee, thanks!" he returned.

While Anna was putting her instrument back in its case, James had turned around on the bench and was watching her. For some time, three weeks to be precise, James had had in his possession an antique mint green velvet box.

For a woman, he assumed, three weeks probably seemed like only a moment in time. But for a man who had much on his mind, it seemed like an eternity.

The velvet box was safely hidden between his T-shirts in the bedroom dresser drawer. It did not weigh much on his mind when Anna was not in the house, but when she was, James felt as if he was keeping an awful secret from her. However, since she knew nothing about his intentions, technically the ring wasn't a secret.

That much he had himself convinced of, but his fingertips danced with worry on his pants leg as he sat.

"Anna," he began, but hesitated, for the next few words could add the right or wrong ingredient to his question. How could he say it without causing too much suspicion? He took in a breath for support and let the words ride on his breath as he let it out.

"I was wondering, well, do you think we work well—together?"

After a moment's pause, she replied, "Yeah, I suppose we do."

James coughed a little to clear his throat.

"I mean, as . . . as a couple."

Putting the violin case next to the front door, Anna

turned her head slightly toward him. A small, innocent smile lifted her lightly freckled cheeks. His heartbeat increased as her smile played uneasily on his mind. He had good reason to worry; for womankind had an extraordinary talent for becoming suspicious over a few casually spoken words.

"You mean, with you on the piano and me on the violin?" she asked, her tone light and amusing.

A wave of heat washed over James, which may have been a first; for he had never experienced such anxiety in which the physical and mental components of his being fell into a sudden state of disrepair. His mouth opened and he felt beyond stupid, for not a single thought circulated in his mind due to his apprehensiveness from his own simple questions.

As far as he was concerned, there wasn't much difference between himself and a cat stuck in a tree. Height and safety were not taken into consideration, but after the summit was reached fear noticed that the earth had disappeared. The branches above and below engulfed him in evening's darkest stage of twilight, and common sense could not guide him back down among the dark limbs. He clung tightly to the tree; fear shook his nerves, and a cold sweat covered his skin.

Anna stood at the open door looking out and said, "You're growing some real nice flowers out there, James. Next year we'll plant twice as many. Maybe add a few rose bushes next to the porch steps so we can enjoy their sweet fragrance."

Realizing he was being spoken to, James stopped tapping his fingers against his legs, put his palms together and placed them between his inner thighs. He sat there on the piano bench feeling again like the little boy who gave away Valentine's Day cards to everyone in his class. He didn't understand why everyone turned and stared at him. He didn't understand why every girl and boy laughed at him, until his teacher pointed out that he had signed every card "Love, Jimmy." No one told him otherwise. But then, what does a seven-year-old know about such things?

And although James was no longer that young boy he was anxious, for he was smitten with Anna, and with Anna alone. What they had was beyond special. He recalled his father's words of advice to him on Thanksgiving Day.

To claim her heart and own it; to enjoy a lifetime of love and companionship he should be asking her *now*. He should excuse himself and slip into his bedroom that could be their room. He would try to hide a grin on his face as he walked across the living room floor. And yes, he would get down on one knee and give Anna the velvet box.

What kind of look would be in her eyes while the little box with little hinges was opening? What would she say? What would she do?

Fear rippled through him again. It wasn't supposed to be like this. Feelings from long ago were not dead, merely napping in his memory. He thought he had known the other Eve, but discovered that time does not necessarily reveal one's true character.

During the past year, James had come to realize that the first Eve was no comparison to Anna. James did not know this at first because years of expectations, companionship, and love were completely crushed by the first Eve. Although it didn't seem possible at the time, as the months swept by he found himself comparing the two women. In his own strange way, he thanked God for changing things, if He did have a hand in it at all.

"James, are you feeling all right? James?"

Anna had come over and sat down next to him. She had placed a hand on his forehead and was saying that he looked a bit pale and felt somewhat clammy.

"James," she asked again, "are you all right? You aren't catching a spring flu, are you?"

His hands, he noticed, were still tightly wedged between his inner thighs, and it occurred to James that he should at least answer her with a shake of his head.

"I hope not," she said in a mildly brisk tone. Anna stood up abruptly and said, "Well, come on then." Picking up the violin case, she appealed to him once more. "*Come on.*"

James rose from the piano bench and followed her to the door. "Where are we going?" he numbly inquired.

"We are getting some fresh air. You are walking me home."

James closed the door behind him.

As they walked along the country road, there was a sweet loveliness to the evening as dusk dropped its soft, gray veil. The warmth from the late May day rose up from the pavement and mixed with the cooling air that drifted on the darkening horizon. The air spoke of sweetness from the young crops about them, and there was no hint of any man-made machine.

Anna held his hand as they walked, and in the fields

around them an orchestra of crickets played. The couple walking along the country road only smiled at each other. They knew music from nature should not be interrupted, and they applauded the musicians with their gratitude of silence. With each step the song diminished in volume until the crickets were silent.

In the growing dusk, a light-colored object moved across the road. It walked in fits and starts, first moving a step, then hesitating, jerking into motion, then hesitating.

"What is it?" James asked.

Anna furrowed her brow in concentration. "I think it's . . ."

They moved closer to the object that was in no hurry to cross the road. "Ah, it's just one of our neighbor's roosters. Kind of looks like the one we had when I was younger."

"Did it end up on a dinner platter?"

Anna laughed. "Almost!"

"Almost?"

"That was the day that 'Fast Eddy' met my mother."

"His name was Fast Eddy? You had a rooster named *Fast Eddy*?" James chuckled. "Oh Lord! I'm dying to hear this one."

Anna laughed with him. "Well, after the school bus had dropped us kids off one day, we made our way up the long driveway towards the house. After a snack of milk and cookies under the grape arbor, we changed our clothes and ended up around the barnyard. It was there that we spotted Fast Eddy in the strangest position. The rooster hung upside down on a wood fence post; his waxy yellow feet bound in baling twine. The poor creature's eyes rolled around in his head and he looked quite sick. We wondered why Fast Eddy being put through such torture? So I went back to the house and asked." Anna paused for breath, then continued her story.

"Mom's reaction suggested that she had forgotten all about the rooster," she went on. Mom said, 'I suppose it's time to take him down.' After releasing him, the poor thing lay in a heap, his eyes rolling somewhere in the back of his head, his parched mouth hanging open. Mom's face had a touch of pity written across it.

"'I hope I didn't kill it,' she half-mumbled. 'But what did he *do*?' I asked. Then Mom's face got all firm and she huffed, 'I just got sick and tired of him mistreating my girls. He had it coming to him!'"

"You see," Anna explained, "mom's girls were her Rhode Island Red hens. Fast Eddy was a handsome white rooster with mallard tail feathers of blue and green that waved through the air as he chased his harem around the barnyard. He would strut around, placing one foot on the ground, the other up against his soft body, take a few steps, pose, a few more steps, pose. Around the hens he paraded in this pose, surveying his rooster kingdom."

Anna could hardly suppress a laugh as she continued, "Then he would play a game with the hens. After carefully picking one out, Fast Eddy literally ran her over, pounced on her back and grabbed the back of her delicate little neck. He shook it and shook it until I think she had a headache. Then the poor hen would get up, stumble around, shake her head to clear it, and run back to her support group. By this time Fast Eddy was already after another hen." Anna strained her eyes at the rooster in the road that was rapidly disappearing into the dark, then looked back at James.

"After regaining his composure after each episode, he would burst out with a 'cock-a-doodle-doo.' That morning mom had had enough 'doodle-doo'. She felt that he needed to take a vacation, take some weight off his feet. After being caught and hung on the fencepost, his male dignity stripped away, he flapped his wings and called for help. His struggle was in vain."

Anna let out a little sigh and smiled. "Far away under the walnut trees in the dirt pools lay the girls. Dusting themselves off and basking in the filtered sun, they enjoyed the unexpected rest."

"Still lying on the ground, Fast Eddy slowly returned to this world. Walking back to the house I heard mom mumble, 'He's no different. No different!'"

Anna leaned in toward James, confessing, "Although I didn't approve of Fast Eddy's tactics, I really don't think he could have helped himself. After all, a rooster is a rooster."

~*~

Anna finished her story a short distance from the McManus mailbox. She squeezed James' warm and comfortable hand which felt so natural in hers, and letting her content eyes fall upon their joining hands, she smiled. It had been a long, long time—years perhaps—since such happiness was part of her life. Anna slowed her pace.

"James," she said in a quiet voice, "let's start

taking walks more often. We have spent such a long time inside. Not that the time spent under your roof wasn't pleasant," she smiled.

The road slowed down under their feet.

"Your friendship has meant a great deal to me," she acknowledged. "More than I ever thought it would."

Anna let go of his hand and walked a few feet away. "Are you as happy as I am, but also scared of what we mean to each other?"

Anna was looking at the horizon that still had not taken every flicker of light from the heavens. She did not turn her head towards him when words from him were absent. James was not entirely sure if he was supposed to answer her, but he realized within a few moments that the feeling between them had not changed.

Still looking at the horizon, she mused, "There aren't many things, other than my music, my job, and my family, that can match the happiness I feel right now. But still, I find myself wide awake in bed at night actually feeling afraid for feeling so happy. Please don't think that it's such a strange thing. I don't feel sorry for myself for what happened years ago, but when things like that happen pure happiness seems to belong to others. Not to me."

James stood behind her, wrapping his arms around her middle, leaning his cheek against hers.

"Sometimes I wonder," she whispered.

"About what?"

"About life."

"What about it?"

Anna's rib cage fell as she sighed.

"I sometimes wonder if life isn't a windshield, and I am the bug hitting it."

James turned Anna around and pressed her body tightly against his.

"Not anymore, my little ladybug. Not anymore."

After long kisses and hugs in the darkness, Anna made her way to the big farmhouse at the end of the long driveway. At the other end, a young man waved to the young woman who could scarcely see him.

And upon reaching her front porch she whispered into the night, "I love you, Pastor James Michael Edwards."

But the young man could not hear her sweet words, for he was heading towards the musicians in the fields, and was heading home.

## CHAPTER 14—HARVEST OF A FOOL

"Says here that we're supposed to have a good harvest this year." Curly announced this bit of news without looking up from the daily newspaper.

"That's what everyone wants to hear, but it's a little while until harvest time, and anything can happen out there," Anna responded.

"True, true."

Curly resumed his reading and pushed his mug toward Anna. She reached for the glass pot behind her and filled it.

"Thanks, love," he hummed instinctively without looking up.

"You bet."

The café usually had a few customers well after the lunch rush. Long-time retired customers like Curly typically could be found at this table or that. But today the place was his alone. Today he could spread the daily paper out anywhere he pleased.

Anna found some paper towels and window cleaner under the counter.

"If you need me, I'll be right outside."

Curly raised his left hand in acknowledgment.

Stepping out to the sidewalk, her skin felt the warmth of the sun under her T-shirt. After wiping the glass door until it sparkled, she moved to the window at one side and saw that her only customer was turning and folding his paper. By the time she had rubbed the paper towel over the words Richard's Café, her backside was more than a little warm. Stepping back into the partial shade next to the door, her scalp continued to radiate heat in the late June sun.

She let her eyes roam up and down the street, observing pedestrians and vehicles. One car drove passed the café and pulled into a spot on the same side, but several shops down. The usual few moments went by before a driver typically got out of their vehicle. Still, no one emerged. Anna could not get a good look at the occupant, for a string of parked cars blocked her view.

A loud pickup truck briefly caught her attention, and as she was turning to go back inside, she noticed a young gal walking briskly and ungracefully on the opposite side of the street. She wore sunglasses and did not glance about her. Her feet were quick to turn and her hands wasted no time in opening the town's tavern door. She was quick—whoever she was.

Anna half turned toward the café door and stopped—then slowly turned and faced the street. The woman's presence, as brief as it had been, was long enough for Anna to notice her beautiful purple leather boots. Anna felt paralyzed for a few minutes as she leaned against the door and was quickly thinking that the gal could not have seen her standing in the doors' recessed entry.

She stepped inside just long enough to tell the cook and Curly that she had something to tend to. By the time Curly turned himself around on the stool, Anna's apron chaotically hung on the coat rack, the door was closed, and she was halfway across the street.

It was odd to touch the tavern's door handle for the first time ever, but now that it was open she felt obligated to pass through it and enter. The door shut behind her. In her blindness, she was aware how bare her presence must have been.

Country music played, a hard, cracking noise startled her, and male voices laughed, cutting through the dark.

As her eyes slowly adjusted to the dim light, she began to make out dark red booths and tables against the left wall. Two older men at the pool table glanced up for the sake of curiosity, and then continued on with their game. The pool table and some bar stools took up the remainder of the space beyond the booths, and to her right was the bar. Yet the bar, the booths, the chairs, and pool table did not contain the gal who wore the purple boots.

A blonde-haired woman in the neighborhood of fifty-something leaned against the counter and put a cigarette into the corner of her mouth. She puckered her lips that were void of color but not lacking lines. Letting a funnel of smoke rise above her, she watched her contribution to the existing smog in the tavern's atmosphere, and finally swung her attention over to

Anna who was still part of the doorway's entrance.

"Gonna stand there all day, or do I gotta send ya an invitation?" the bartender snapped in a voice roughened by years of nicotine.

Glancing at the booths for a moment, Anna decided to chance it at the bar. Coming over to her, the bartender held a paper coaster between two fingers of her left hand while holding the cigarette in her right.

"What'll ya have?"

Her irksome stare annoyed Anna, and her utter dislike for the callous woman formed minutes ago.

The bartender raised her eyebrows and sighed.

"I'll have a glass of blush wine, please."

Contorting her brows further, the bartender repeated, "A glass of wine? Not a beer? No whiskey? Just a glass of wine?" She seemed dumbfounded by the request.

Anna leaned her arms against the counter.

"Unless my hearing is failing me, I do believe I heard myself ask for a glass of wine. Not a lousy bottle of beer, not a stinking glass of whiskey, but a nice glass of *chilled* wine."

The woman behind the counter hadn't moved the coaster from her fingers.

"Got any?" Anna raised her eyebrows as well.

The coaster was released and landed near Anna. A glass of blush wine was placed on it, but the glass did not produce any moisture on its exterior.

"Excuse me, but could I have some wine that has been *chilled*?"

The bartender looked at Anna, took a drag from her cigarette, and slowly let out a mouthful of smoke.

Although it wasn't aimed directly at her, it may as well have been.    Anna did not want to give the woman the satisfaction of a coughing fit, but she couldn't help herself.

The blonde grinned in pleasure.

When the smoke and coughing passed, Anna hardened her face and dug her eyes into the bartender's.

"I take that as, 'No ma'am, we do not, but I could put a piece of ice in your glass for you'. And, if you do that again with that cigarette, I swear I'll clobber you."

The bartender broke out in a fit of deep, hoarse laughter, turned away and coughed into the ice bin, and setting a cup of ice next to the wine glass, rearranged the lines on her face. She watched the younger woman drop the slick pieces into the glass, and spreading a hand out on her left hip, she spoke again.

"You do that and you don't like it, you're payin' for it."

Anna held the glass up and swirled it a few times. Moisture slowly appeared on the exterior.

"That'll be three fifty."

"Three fifty for a lousy glass of wine?"

"Two fifty for the wine. A buck for the ice." The bartender smirked.

Anna leaned back and produced a handful of one dollar bills and a lottery ticket from her pants pocket, putting it all back except for four dollars. She placed the money on the counter and as the bartender closed in on it, Anna plucked away two and put them back in her pocket.

The bartender extended her arms and placed her hands on her edge of the counter.

"I *said* three-fifty."

Anna shook her head.

The older woman straightened herself and said in an ill attempt at humor, "My mistake about the ice. You still owe me fifty cents."

"You're right. *Your* mistake."

The bartender thought she could grab the glass of wine and throw it at Anna, but her move was anticipated. Anna shook her head slowly, and backing off, the bartender began flirting with the two men at the pool table.

Taking a cautious sip, Anna noticed that the blonde had her backside toward her. Placing the glass placed on the coaster, she quietly slipped off the stool, passed the pool table, and stood in the dimly lit hallway unnoticed. The Men's and Ladies' restrooms were side by side on her left, with the Ladies' the farthest away. Pausing against the wall, Anna was grateful that the three people around the pool table were making such a racket as they cussed and yelled at each other for fun. Anna thought of going directly in, but as she stood in the poorly lit, narrow hallway she thought she heard muffled voices. She placed an ear against the door and the voices were indeed coming from the Ladies' Room.

Even before her hand touched the door, her heartbeat was already accelerating. The sound of heavy moaning and deep crying grew louder as the door was opened no further than a crack, revealing nearly all flesh. Repetitive "Oh, shits" and "Oh, Gods," were expelled in painful quivering cries from the female leaning against the counter while holding the faucet. The female who wore the beautiful purple boots wore a strap of sorts around her waist and hips. She was grabbing the flesh of the other, and with speed and force thrust her pelvis in a rapid back and forth rhythm, slapping the butt of the other female so hard the other cried in pain while cussing and begging for more. Had they not been engaged in such deep physical passion, the participants might have noticed that the door was ajar and that there was woman on the other side who was experiencing feelings that were entirely new to her. Her face was warm and her heart was beating wildly. Suddenly, something jolted her to attention. Her body froze, her heart stopped, and a thin layer of cool sweat surfaced, all in a split second. She scanned the dim hallway. The moment of panic passed, and Anna softly closed the door and let out a sigh of relief.

Letting out a deep, slow breath, she emerged from the hallway and resumed her seat at the bar. She took no notice of the bartender who was smoking, slowly wiping down the counter with a bar towel, edging her way over to her. Anna was swirling the watered down wine and was staring at the glass, deep in thought.

"Did you like what you saw, honey?" the bartender whispered without looking at Anna. "Never took you for the girl-on-girl type."

Anna lifted her eyes to see that the blonde was working her gross tongue around inside her wrinkly mouth.

"Ya' must've liked somethin' 'cause your cheeks are 'bout the same color as your wine when you started drinkin' it." She snickered unpleasantly as she watched to see how Anna would react.

Anna kept swirling the liquid in the glass.

As if the bartender hadn't spoken, Anna said, "I want to know if the occupants of the Ladies' Room come here often. Say, on a particular day of the week?"

The bartender smiled.

Putting the glass down on the counter, Anna looked at her with a knowing grin. "I'll make it worth your while."

Reaching inside her jeans pocket, she separated the dollar bills and took out the lottery ticket. She held it up in front of her and the bartender reached out for it, but Anna kept it just out of her reach.

"It's good for Wednesday. Worth 13 *million*. In two days you could be the richest bartender around." Anna paused. "What do you say?"

The woman crushed her cigarette in a glass ashtray, and a small line of smoke escaped from the remains. She stared at the cigarette butt and finally answered, "I think I'd be the richest ex-bartender not living 'round here. I wouldn't bother scrapin' this place off my shoes! I'd take 'em off and throw 'em in the dumpster out back, and then I'd walk barefoot to my car and get the hell out of this town."

Anna gave a sarcastic questioning grin as she held up the lottery ticket again.

Leaning against the counter where countless bottles of liquor stood, the bartender folded her arms under her chest and almost squinted at the small piece of paper. Her facial muscles moved and her eyes narrowed. Her thoughts moved quickly.

"They come twice a week," the woman began, but she interrupted herself by casting a cautious eye to her right. When there was no sound or sight of anyone emerging from the back rooms, the blonde found her tongue. Leaning forward, she whispered, "But *always* on Mondays."

"What time?"

"At one."

"Always?"

The bartender nodded and snatched the ticket from Anna.

Her errand completed, Anna started to leave when the woman blurted out, "I can see why my ex-husband called you a 'spit' of a thing."

Anna turned back to the woman.

"Huh?"

"You kicked him out of your daddy's place one day."

"Oh, so *that* was your husband. Yes, I remember him. He thought I was being a little too bitchy for having PMS that day. I didn't like him, so yes, I threw him out."

"Good thing I wasn't there," huffed the bartender. "Things would have been a little different."

Anna chuckled. "Don't think so."

The blonde made a threatening move in her direction, but Anna departed from the bartender's jagged personality, and from the dark, smoky room that she despised but lived her life in. The brightness of the afternoon immediately blinded her, and the warmth on her body felt wonderful as she slowly made her way back across and down the street. She was only partly aware of vehicles and pedestrians around her. Such things were insignificant to her at the moment.

Curly was still waiting on his stool at the counter

with a scowl reserved especially for her. He faced the door with crossed arms tight against his chest and tucked his jaw into his thick neck. He watched her roam aimlessly about the café while she rubbed her hands together and released tension from her knuckles. It did not take Curly long to figure out that the young woman who left some time ago was not the same one who had come back.

Anna paced around the Formica counter where Curly sat, thumping her fingers at wild speed along its length. Although he was annoyed at being left alone in the café for such a long time, his initial irritation was now replaced by worry.

"All right! That's enough! No more pacin' around. Just watchin' you is tuckerin' me out!"

Anna stood by the door for a few moments, and then to Curly's surprise, she flipped the café sign on the door to the side which read, "I'm Sorry We're Closed, Please Come Again". She walked backwards, staggering slightly, and put her hands out to feel for the counter or a stool. Her eyes appeared worthless to her, for perhaps they wanted to take part in the secrecy that only her brain knew about for the moment.

"My friend," he said in a deep, careful voice, "what'cha hidin' in that head of yours?"

"Oh, Curly . . . oh, Curly!"

"Oh, Curly *what*!"

Anna turned to the older man and looked at him blankly with her mouth agape for a long moment.

"Curly, I don't know if it's fate or opportunity or what, but they have just offered me a plate of sweet revenge. Without even having bitten into it, I can taste it, and it is *good*. I don't think I should push it away."

"What the heck are you talkin' about?" Curly sputtered.

He never had seen such gleam in her eyes or the strange, calculating expression her face wore. "I didn't think of myself as being the sort of person who has vindictive blood, but then one cannot know what one cannot see."

Anna's fingers pounced on the counter top that kept pace with her thoughts. It was more than Curly could handle.

"Damn it, woman, sit on those things! Now what in God's name are you talk'n 'bout?"

"Oh, Curly, you're a good friend of mine, but I can't tell you just yet, for I don't even know myself what to do with this. I must think this out carefully, for I believe such an opportunity like this will come only once. There is much to plan and do, but I must take care." She paused, then added mysteriously, "I have never been friends with the devil and don't intend to start now."

Curly shook his head and poked a thick finger at her head. "I don't know what's goin' on in that head of yours, but it don't sound good."

Anna smiled at him and placed a hand on his shoulder. "Curly, it's going to be all right. It's going to be *all* right, but I must ask you to leave, for as I said, there are things I must do."

Poor Curly departed from the café shaking his head. The cook was paid for a full day and was sent home early, too.

The café was cleaned in a hurry, the door was shut

and the key turned in the lock. Anna stood outside and looked down and across the street at the tavern's door. Her heart was anxious, her soul was skeptical, and her mind was far ahead of her feet. Several folks passed by the young woman who stood there in the sun. Their stares went unnoticed.

Her backbone was straight, and many years of sorrow written upon her face were close to being released. Knowing that the day of reckoning was near made her body feel light, and the happiness that was almost hers depended upon one thing—her plan working without a glitch.

~*~

The bartender was in the middle of fixing a whiskey sour when the door leading to the street opened. Pausing briefly, a handsome woman with long auburn hair came in and smoothly glided into one of the booths.

Delivering the drink to a customer who was playing pool, she eyed the female in slight jealousy and contempt, for many seasons had passed since her own youth.

The young woman had attracted glances from every male in the tavern, but she seemed to take no notice. This in itself infuriated the older woman, for her type knew how to manipulate men by taking advantage of their natural longings.

The dim lights in the room gently brushed over the young woman's thick, wavy hair that parted on her shoulder blades and rested on her noticeably well-endowed chest.

Because she sat facing the door, the bartender was able to cross the floor and give her a cold stare without worrying about being noticed. Turning toward the girl, a pleasant grin was cemented in place, but upon seeing the pretty, sweet face of the stranger, the grin straightened and cracked. Leaning against the booth she tucked the round serving tray under an arm, then once more attempted a pleasant expression.

"You're not from 'round here, are ya?"

The eyes of the young woman casually lifted to hers and they seemed to sparkle. Her smile was warm and friendly as she told the bartender that she was from Seattle on business, and would be visiting a friend while passing through town.

While the out-of-towner mentioned that her friend would be joining her shortly, the door to the street opened and then closed. She did not look at the two females as they walked passed the bar to place their customary token of gratitude on the counter.

"Just to let ya know," the older woman began, "the Girls' Room is being cleaned and won't be open for at least half-an-hour."

The pretty girl smiled and nodded, then asked, "Could I bother you for a nice glass of ice water?" She opened her purse, produced some lipstick, and carefully applied it without the aid of a mirror. Then, removing her little wallet, she took out a crisp fifty-dollar bill, folded it, and gestured with a manicured finger at the bartender.

Through her eyelashes, her playful, soft eyes rose to meet those of the blonde woman, and while the pretty girl tucked the bill in one of the bartender's jean pockets, a delicate pink tip of a tongue played on her soft upper lip and her eyes had turned seductive as she tapped the bill down with a delicate finger.

"Will *that* be sufficient?" she asked in a pleasing voice.

"Sure," the bartender ventured, sounding anything but sure.

While she went behind the bar and found a glass, the door to the street opened and closed. This time a dark haired, plump, middle-aged woman stood in the dim light and began to look around.

Upon seeing the newcomer at the door, the girl in the booth fluttered her delicate painted fingertips in the air to get her attention. The dark-haired woman quickly eyed the young lady across from her. There was something familiar about her, but this young lady had long auburn hair, was pretty, and dressed quite the opposite of another young girl whom she vaguely resembled in stature.

The older woman extended a hand across the table where it was suspended awkwardly for a few moments. She thought she noticed a twitch leaving the young woman's mouth, but then a hand that revealed long red nails rose to meet hers. As flesh touched flesh, she twitched again, but the sweet smile did not leave her face.

"Hello, my name is Katherine. You'll have to forgive me, it's been a long drive and I'm somewhat exhausted."

The plump woman smiled. "Of course, dear. I'm sure you are very tired from your trip."

"I had no idea, Mrs. Barker that it took so long to travel across this state of ours."

"Please, call me Faith. I cannot tell you how

anxious I am to learn more about Pastor Edwards. He has not heeded my advice . . . well, let's just say I may need a little help outside the boundaries of Eastern Washington."

The younger woman smiled and smoothed her hair. "I am more than *happy* to help you deal with James. He turned my life upside down after he fathered our son. I told him that we must be married and that he should be responsible for his actions. But, to my complete surprise, he said that he was engaged to be married. I found out later that he left town without being engaged to anyone at all."

Mrs. Barker arranged an expression of shocked disbelief on her own features. "You *poor* thing! But I'm curious about something. We spoke so little on the phone that I'm not sure if you mentioned how you got my—"

The bartender finally arrived with the glass of water and the conversation stopped. The dark-haired woman was asked if she wanted anything, but the only acknowledgement the blonde received was a shake of her head. Just as she was turning to leave the two women alone, she heard the pretty young thing say, "Madam—will you not take this with you?"

The bartender turned around to see that a paper coaster was being held between the girl's lovely painted fingernails, and to her delight the coaster was brought to soft colored lips and she heard a faint parting of the lips. Her eyes rose and gazed upon the soft eyes of the girl and then she heard her demand, "Take this now, bitch, and leave us alone."

Without a word, she took the coaster, and casually

walking back to the bar counter, she read what was on it. "When I look at YOU and nod, GO to the Men's Room. I'll follow. I want you BAD."

Mrs. Barker cleared her throat suddenly. Turning her attention back to the older woman, Katherine saw a very startled expression waiting for her. She wiggled her figure and giggled, "Oh, I love doing that! It gives me such a—*rush* when I can boss people around."

Mrs. Barker's expression changed from shock to intrigue as she inclined her dark head and grinned. "I can't say I've ever used that word before."

There was a slight pause.

The young lady pretended to pout and replied, "Wouldn't you agree with me Faith, that there are a certain class of people that deserve the word *bitch*?" She paused and raised her eyebrows. "Because, if you don't agree with me, I don't see how you and I could ever be friends."

"Katherine, you little darling!" the woman cried. "We are kindred spirits! Our hearts, our minds, our souls, and our thoughts are one!" She grabbed the girl's hands and squeezed them. "But please, you were about to tell me something before the—*bitch* interrupted us."

Katherine smiled, then examined a glossy fingernail as she purred, "Well, I never used to believe in fate, but as of last weekend I may have been converted. You see, for a while I hadn't been going to church, but last Sunday there was a little voice speaking to me." She looked directly into Mrs. Barker's eyes.

"'Katherine,' it whispered, 'I have lost one of my precious lambs. You have strayed from the flock and I am sad that one of my own is missing.' Obviously, God

Himself was speaking to me, so I went to the nearest church I could find." Shifting slightly in her booth, she continued. "Well, sitting next to me was a nice couple, and after studying them for a while, I realized that the husband looked like James in a way. So after the service was over, I introduced myself and found out that their last name was Edwards. After that I couldn't help but ask if they had a son named James, which of course they did. I told them I was an old friend of his, and casually asked where he was living these days. When I mentioned that I would like to pay him a surprise visit, I asked Mrs. Edwards for the phone number of his church. She didn't know off the top of her head, so she suggested calling the church's secretary to get directions. I did, and I also asked her to pick a name from the congregation, and she picked yours."

"That's interesting that they would still have my phone number," mused Mrs. Barker.

"Why is that?" Katherine asked inquisitively.

"Let's just say that Pastor Edwards and I have had a falling out, and now I attend services . . . elsewhere."

"I see."

"So, Katherine, what do you want to do?" Mrs. Barker's question nearly sang with excitement.

The young woman's eyes locked onto the older woman's eyes, and a nasty grin stretched across her mouth.

"I want revenge. I want to make life so horrible for this person, that they'll wish they were—dead."

Mrs. Barker smiled an even nastier grin and gushed, "I like you Katherine! You're just what I've been looking for."

Subsequently, there was pleasure in this scheme for Katherine, which caused her to smile, and letting out a sigh, she tilted her pretty head to the left, glanced at something and nodded.

"I am only too happy to help. But first—if I may draw something to your attention . . ."

The older woman sat still for a moment, then asked, "I hope I don't have lipstick on my teeth, do I?"

The young lady gently smiled in sympathy and gave a small nod.

"I'm afraid I was in too much of a hurry leaving the house," Mrs. Barker offered as she searched deep into her purse for a tissue, and after having found one, she rubbed it against her front teeth, running her tongue over them as well.

"Is it gone, my dear?"

The young woman sweetly smiled and shook her lovely head again. "Might I suggest a visit to the Ladies' Room? It looks like it might be past the pool table and down the hallway," she offered helpfully.

Scooting to the edge of the seat, the plump woman stood up.

"Now, don't go anywhere. We have so much to discuss," she giggled. "I'll only be a moment."

"Don't worry about me. I'm not going anywhere," the young lady half-purred.

Katherine quickly turned and looked across the room at the bar. She thought her peripheral vision had seen the bartender go. She was right. The woman in the booth breathed deeply and whispered to herself, "I wouldn't dream of going anywhere. Wait, wait . . . one, two, three. . ."

Abruptly, a horrific ear-piercing shriek filled the tavern followed by the high-pitched screams of younger females as well. Beer bottles dropped and shattered on the cement floor as the tavern's patrons froze, their petrified eyes flaring.

And from the depths of a mother's soul, a horrible, agonizing, groaning cry burst like a colossal facial zit in the air. In desperation, the dark-haired woman tried to escape what she just had witnessed, fleeing passed the pool table and the booths and the bar. And while in flight, Katherine's laughter filled her ears while she flung herself out the door, into her car, and with haste drove away from the tavern.

The Author of Rumors shook her head frantically as if a swarm of hornets were attacking her. Their high-pitched, annoying sounds were embedded within the woman's head, and flashes of her daughter and of her trusty accomplice felt like they were cracking her skull open. A torrent of tears did not care if they spilled onto her blouse, and therefore she did not see any stop signs. Alas, it was not her time, so fate was postponed and held its hand back for the moment.

However, back in the tavern's Ladies' Room, the occupants were not in hysterics of embarrassment, but were laughing scornfully, being evermore insolent and reckless, regardless of consequences, for they had decided it was time to face the nemesis of peoples' bigotry towards them.

~*~

His body was draped over his favorite chair as he rested his eyes, but the sound of a familiar truck opened them and he lifted his head off the cushion. It occurred to James that it was early afternoon. There was only one other time when Anna closed up early in the afternoon—and that was when the Quiet Man passed away. His heart sank and he hoped another customer hadn't died in the café.

Before he could get up and open the door for her, a stranger rushed in and stood in his living room. His eyes took her all in, from her beautiful bouncy hair which rested on lovely breasts, her pretty, perfectly made-up face, her gleaming nail polish and stylish clothes. James had been looking at her face, but it was her eyes that he took notice of. He placed his hands on the soft arms of the chair and slowly rose.

"*Anna?*"

The auburn-haired young woman raised a hand over her head and slowly removed the beautiful wig, dangling it at her side.

"Anna, what . . . what the hell!?" he managed to get out.

"I'm—I'm leaving town for a few days," she announced to the living room.

James had his mouth open and then shook his head in total bewilderment. "Wait a minute! Where are you going, and why?" he demanded.

"I suppose I'll need to tell dad that I won't be at the café for a few days . . . pack some things. . . get money at the bank . . . put gas . . . in the truck," she rambled on, almost absentmindedly.

James grabbed her shoulders and shook them, still trying to absorb what was going on.

"Anna! Anna!"

She started to laugh hysterically. "You should have

been there. Oh, I wish you could have seen me!"

As James was telling Anna to sit down on the couch, he had guided her to it and pushed her down onto the cushions. He held onto her arms and knelt before her.

"I was so damn nervous and scared I thought I'd throw up! I wish you could have heard the screaming. I did it, James! I did it!" Her laugh turned exultant. "I was so afraid that she would recognize me. But the stupid woman didn't!"

"Anna! Anna! You're scaring me. Talk to me!" James demanded.

"I hope God doesn't hold what I did against me. What is done is done," Anna mussed decisively.

James removed his hands from her arms and stretched his fingers around her head and brought her face just inches from his.

"Anna, look at me!" he growled, demanding her immediate attention. His voice quivered with fear.

Her eyes finally rested on his, and he was scared at what he saw. He didn't want to know, but he had to ask. "Anna, please tell me that you didn't hurt anybody."

"Hurt who?"

His grip tightened on her face and he wanted to shout at her.

"Did you kill someone?" James hotly demanded.

Anna's eyes opened wider and her lashes fluttered wildly. "Ow—you're hurting me! James, you're hurting me!"

He did not release his grip. "Answer me. Did you *kill* someone?"

"No!" she answered with a repulsed tone in her

voice. "For heaven's sake, you silly man, why would I do a stupid thing like that?"

Relief flooded through him, making him weak in the knees. "Well, you tell me! What am I supposed to think when this stranger comes through my door, takes off her wig and starts talking as if she's gone out of her mind?"

"Do I look like a murderer?" Anna said with a look of injured innocence.

James flushed. "No, but who's to say what a murderer looks like?" He paused and removed his hands from her face. "I'm sorry, but what is going on?"

Anna looked him square in the eye. "I'm a woman who got to dish out some revenge. I wouldn't say that we're even for all that she's done, but that's all right. I can live with that. Just knowing that I was able to cause her some pain has made me the happiest person in the world."

"Anna McManus . . . why do you have to be damn frustrating?"

Anna let out a heavy sigh. "I'll explain everything when I get back."

"And just where do you think you're going?" he inquired.

"I don't know. Maybe I'll see what Seattle is like."

He shook his head, and then marked the words for distinction. "So, you are planning on leaving now, which would put you in a strange city after dark, and you don't have the foggiest idea what Seattle is like. Anna, you're not going anywhere," James said sternly.

"I beg your pardon?" her voice rose in slightly defiance.

"Not unless I come with you."

Anna looked at him with sudden amazement. "Okay, let's go!"

"In the morning," he reasoned.

"I don't want to wait until morning!" Anna objected impatiently.

"You're going to have to if you want to go to Blakely Island."

Anna stared at him in further astonishment. "Blakely? You mean the island you talked about months ago?"

"Yes. But I need to make a few arrangements to see if my buddy can fly us there. So, if you want to go to the island, stay put!"

~*~

James was deep in thought as he absentmindedly paced the kitchen floor while sipping coffee as he waited for Anna's arrival. He had been thinking and worrying of his hastily made decision the day before to accompany Anna—a single woman, on a middle-of-the-week, out-of-town, excursion.

As a pastor, he knew that what he was about to do was not right. His common sense nagged him and told him that he should not be doing this. The sudden "excuse" of leaving town was communicated on the church's office assistant's answering machine, alluding, "that a friend of his was stealing him away for a few days."

As a man—a single man—his conscience greatly weighed on him. And what about Anna's parents? What must they be thinking! James let his chin drop against his chest and he sighed through partially open lips. Mr. and Mrs. McManus. Oh, Lord! James sighed again. He expected a call from them, and nervously waited, and waited—but the phone was silent. He pressed his eyes shut, arched his eyebrows, and shook his head at Anna's familiar stubbornness, for he knew without a doubt that she would take off to some unknown destination without him, and James suspected, that her parents knew that as well. His chuckle turned into a throaty growl, which was emitted into the morning air as he accepted this resignation with a wry grin. They would go together.

At 7:00 sharp, Anna knocked on his door and placed her duffle bag beside his in the living room. She had been instructed to bring a duffle bag, instead of a suitcase, as they conformed nicely within the tail section of single-engine airplane. James was just finishing his coffee when she joined him in the kitchen.

"Are you ready?" he asked after he washed and dried his cup.

"I still can't believe we're going," Anna exclaimed in excited disbelief.

"Believe it. I can't wait to show you all around the island. Wiley says we can use the truck if we want."

"Wiley?"

"Wiley Martin. Now, if you could just wait outside for a few minutes so I'm not distracted . . ."

Anna wait on the front porch while James double checked every room to ensure that appliances were unplugged, and timers for lamps were set to go on in the evening, and off in the morning. The front door was closed and locked. Their duffle bags were loaded in the back of his truck, and smiling at Anna, he brought the truck to life, and they set off down the road heading west.

Miles and miles of wheat fields occupied the space of the rear view mirror. Anna leaned her head against the window and let the wind roll into the cab through a slight opening between metal and glass. Her eyelids were lowered and pieces of hair caught the wind here and there. James kept glancing over at her.

"You're looking at me, aren't you?"

James had to laugh. "How can you tell?"

"Every time you turn your head, your neck muscles kind of pop."

James wished that Anna could reach over and give his neck and shoulders a massage, but she looked too comfortable to leave her spot against the door.

James had not forgotten about the events of the day before and he wanted her to tell him everything. Of course, if she were anything like him, she would not want questions thrown at her at such an early hour in the morning. His questions would have to wait, and he was sure that sometime during the day she would tell him.

They headed west on Highway 26 and James realized that it had been almost a year and a half since he had traveled in the other direction. They passed Palouse Falls, Othello, and Royal City. James remembered stopping there for gas and coffee, and he remembered reading the letter from his aunt and uncle. Had it really been sixteen months since that day? James shook his head.

"What's the matter?" Anna asked.

"Huh?"

"You just shook your head."

"Oh, I was just thinking."

"Are you changing your mind about this trip?"

"No. I was just thinking about the last city back there."

"Care to think out loud?"

"I will, but first, you're going to tell me everything that happened yesterday. Then, you can read the letter that brought me here, in a manner of speaking. It should still be in the glove box."

Anna had her hand on the latch of the glove box, and reaching over, James gave her arm a swat.

"Ouch! You hit me!" She rubbed her arm looking surprised and cross.

"Rightly so!" he returned. "You haven't spilled your guts yet. Come on. No details, no letter."

While Anna started at the very beginning, leaving nothing out, Highway 26 changed into Interstate 90. Surprisingly, James' reaction to Anna's scheme that was carried out on Mrs. Barker wasn't what she expected. There was no verbal chastisement whatsoever, only an occasional hard glance, more than a few raised eyebrows, some head shaking, and looks of pure shock. After she finished her account of connected events that placed her in his living room the day before, silence hung in the cab and she thought it best not to interfere with it. In the absence of words, James' wry grin and shaking of his head led her to hope, that for the sake of peace on their first outing, it would not benefit him at all if he were to shred her rationale and conduct like a cocktail napkin.

They stopped at Ellensburg for lunch and

continuing west again. Anna was allowed to read the letter. When she was done, the letter was carefully placed back in the envelope and tucked away in the glove box. She was quiet, looking out the window at the dry landscape around them.

Anna admitted in a soft tone of voice, "I think your aunt and uncle made a good choice."

James' attention had been focused on the road, and glancing at her briefly, he made a "Huh?" sound.

"Your aunt and uncle . . . I'm glad they decided to ask you to watch over their little flock. Had you declined their offer, one little lamb would never have met you."

James reached over, held her hand, and gave it a squeeze. They drove for many miles holding hands in silence, but their thoughts, which were many, were drawn from wells deep within their memories.

As they drew closer to the Snoqualmie National Forest, Anna grew more and more excited with Mount Rainier coming into view. She sat on the edge of her seat with her mouth agape and her eyes sparkling, taking in the new wonders about her.

"I had no idea the rest of Washington was this beautiful," she sighed.

James glanced over at Anna after he heard a little sniffle coming from her direction. He smiled at her and she smiled back, and he noticed that her eyes were moistened from explicable happiness.

Part way over the mountain pass, much-needed leg stretching, shoulder massaging, and more leg stretching were due. Anna asked if she could drive for a while, and James was more than happy to be the passenger so he could rest.

Before they entered Eastgate James thought it would be safer if he drove, since Anna's attention might not be completely on the growing traffic. He was right. They made it over the I-90 floating bridge, and they made it only because Anna was not at the wheel. Her head was busy whipping this way and that, catching glimpses of new things everywhere. She excitedly threw question after question at him, and he was happy to explain the sights to her. As they got off the bridge, James couldn't help but wonder what she was feeling as she took in Seattle for the first time.

As for him, it felt strange. It had been many, many months since he had driven through the busy streets that had been his home, and now, as he maneuvered through the hectic traffic, he almost wished he were back on the quiet roads that cut through brown and gold wheat fields on the other sides of the mountains.

At last they reached their destination. James turned the tired truck into the Boeing Field Airport parking lot and let out a painful moan while trying to get his legs out of the truck and plant them on the ground.

"You owe me a long massage. I don't think my body will ever be the same!"

"I feel fine," grinned Anna. "Maybe I should drive going back home."

"Can I hold you to that?" James bent his aching body sideways, forwards and backwards before adding, "We definitely need to stop more often on the way back. Speaking of backs . . . boy, am I looking forward to that massage!"

Anna shook her head, smiling. "If you're done

complaining, shouldn't we see if Wiley is here?"

Anna had barely finished her sentence when a man approached the high chain link fence.

"Jimmy! Is that you?"

With the fence in between them, James introduced Anna to his buddy Wiley Martin. James' friend was a clean-cut, ordinary looking guy, and there was a twinkle in his eye as he looked at his friend who had a hand around the waist of the woman who stood next to him.

James and Anna were let in through a gate and followed Wiley passed a few rows of single and twin-engine airplanes.

Wiley spoke, addressing Anna. "James tells me that you've never been on this side of the state."

Anna nodded. "It's true."

She waited for him to laugh, but instead he winked at her and whispered, "If James hadn't keep you all to himself these past months, I would have flown you over here and kept you for myself."

"I heard that!" James said in a mock-serious tone.

Although Anna's cheeks were deep pink with embarrassment, she couldn't hold back her laughter.

Wiley pointed to his Mooney and asked Anna if she had ever been in a small airplane.

Anna shook her head.

Wiley appeared to come to a decision. "In that case, I think you need to sit next to me, so I can show you how to fly this thing."

James thought that Anna would have jumped at the chance, but instead she protested saying that they probably had a lot of catching up to do, and it would prove difficult unless James sat up front. Actually, had it not been her first flight, she gladly would have taken up his offer. She really just wanted to sit by herself and look down on the sparkling blue water of Puget Sound; its surface dotted with innumerable islands, large and small, ranging from a mere speck upon the water to the largest, Whidbey Island.

After everyone had settled in and the duffle bags were tucked in behind Anna, Wiley brought the plane to life. Both men wore headsets so they could communicate with the airport tower and speak to each other. Over the noise of the engine, Anna thought she heard Wiley ask the tower for permission for take off.

There were a few planes practicing landings and takeoffs, so it was just a matter of minutes until the plane lined up to the runway heading north.

She could hear Wiley say something else to the tower, and then the plane quickly rolled forward and roared with power. In a matter of seconds it seemed like the plane was airborne. Anna found herself holding onto safety handles because, as the plane gained altitude, it bumped up and down.

Anna noticed a chart in a pocket behind the pilot's seat. Folding it out, she found their location. Elliott Bay was below them, and to her right she saw downtown Seattle with its tall buildings that her younger sister would love. And then there was the Space Needle that was constructed for the 1962 World's Fair.

Flying over the water made Anna a little more nervous than she wanted to admit. She was glad that James did not look back to ask how she was doing. She noticed that he and Wiley were constantly looking out the windows. James pointed at something and Anna looked in that direction. Above them and to their right was another small plane heading towards Boeing Field. James turned around and told Anna that one of the most important jobs of a passenger is to help spot other aircraft for the pilot. Anna smiled and nodded. Now she had a job that would keep her eyes occupied on the sky rather than on the blue water far below.

James turned around again and pointed to a long island on their left. He explained that they couldn't cut across Whidbey Island because they had to keep a certain distance from the Naval Air Station.

Pieces of land emerged from the water, but as the afternoon sun shone down on it, it blinded Anna's eyes and it took more than a few moments to recover her sight. Then she remembered her sunglasses in her bag. As they neared the San Juan Islands, Wiley descended a few hundred feet so they were closer to the beautiful scenery. Anna wondered which island was theirs, and as Wiley reduced power and descended she saw a small, forested island rising to meet them. The sparkling water seemed to greet them too quickly, and looking ahead of her, there was a little runway that cut through the trees. Suddenly the plane bounced hard and Wiley hollered back to her.

"Cross winds! Hold on tight!"

The plane, she noticed, was coming in slightly sideways. Anna said a few prayers as the plane swayed and bounced from one direction to another. But then the wheels touched down and the plane taxied slowly down the runway. After letting out a huge sigh, Anna's heart still would not calm down.

Suddenly, there was a brown flash in front of them,

and quickly turning her head, Anna saw a small deer run off the runway and stop in the yard in front of a cabin. James explained that deer are notorious for crossing the runway, and can be dangerous to a plane and its passengers if struck. Anna hadn't noticed the cabins and little houses at first. Nor did she notice a simple paved road in the shape of a racetrack on the outskirts of the runway.

Between the road and the forest a line of little houses and cabins faced west, and on the other side of the runway, with their front doors facing east, more cabins sat in the shade of fir trees. While the plane came to a stop on the side of the road, Anna could see that no two dwellings were alike.

The men took off their headsets, and turning around in his seat, Wiley smiled and said, "Welcome to Blakely Island. Sorry about the approach. That end of the runway gets some pretty bad winds and we've had a few accidents because of it."

Just when her heart was beginning to calm down, he had to mention that.

The first thing Anna noticed when she stepped out of the plane was the wonderful air smelling of salt water and fir forest, and the fir trees in which the birds sang seemed to reach amazingly high up into the clear blue sky.

James gathered the duffle bags and thanked his friend with a strong handshake. Wiley told James that the key to the cabin was still in the same place, the fishing tackle was still in the garage, and the truck should have enough gas in it to explore the upper roads.

Wiley then reached out his hand to Anna and gave

it a little squeeze. He said that he was very happy to have met James' lady friend, he hoped she would have a wonderful time, and in two days, come Thursday morning, he would return.

With that, he climbed back into the Mooney and headed for the taxiway. After waving to Wiley and watching him disappear from their sight, James picked up the duffle bags and headed down a road into the sun. Anna tried taking her bag back, stating that it was hers and that she was perfectly able to carry it. James only shook his head and said that she could not win this one.

"During your stay here, it's only fair to tell you that chivalry reigns on this island!" he said with a grin.

"I'm not sure if I could get used to that," Anna politely countered.

"Get used to it," replied James.

As they neared the end of the narrow road, Anna could see more cabins nestled between patches of trees. The sun darted behind every tree and followed them as they made a right turn down a one-lane dirt road.

"It's not much farther. Just five or six houses down. You probably can't see it until we get closer."

As they walked along, Anna drank the air in gulps.

"Save some for me," James laughed.

"I can't help it; it is so wonderful here. In a way I envy you, for all the times you said you've been here." Anna inhaled deeply again, her eyes closed with pleasure.

"Well, I can't fix the past, but Wiley said we can visit whenever we want to."

"Wiley said that?" she gasped.

James nodded.

Anna stopped suddenly. "Oh, James, you mean we can come here again, and again?"

"Well, only if you want to," he teased.

She planted herself in front of him and grabbed his shirt.

"Don't hurt me!" he pleaded, half-closing his eyes, not knowing what to expect. She tugged on his shirt, and lowering his face a bit, Anna kissed him warmly on the lips.

"I'll take that as a 'yes'."

He swung a duffle bag in the direction of a dirt driveway. "Here it is."

The fir trees thinned themselves out, and all but a handful stood close to a rustic cabin that was a safe distance from the jagged west edge of the island. A few paces away from the lodging was a garage that looked much like the cabin.

James set the duffle bags down on the small front entryway, and told Anna he would go around the house and get the key that was under a rock next to one of the trees.

Upon entering the cabin, James turned on the lights and immediately opened every curtain. The daylight revealed a cozy room that consisted of a kitchen on the left with a small table and four chairs under a window. Beyond the kitchen on the south wall was a fireplace made from round river rock, which extended to the pointed ceiling. Situated in the center of the cabin was the living room, which was spacious enough to hold a small sofa, two lounge chairs that flanked the fireplace, end tables and several lamps. To the right were two bedrooms with the bathroom in between. But the best features of all were the French doors and windows that took up nearly the entire length of the wall. Lastly, above the doors was a cozy loft with windows so sunsets could be gazed upon.

Anna looked at the fireplace again and wondered if James was planning on building a fire in the evening. If he wasn't, she would.

After the inspection, she found James unpacking in one of the two bedrooms. Her room was the same as the other with a queen-size bed, a dresser with mirror above it, a wooden chair in one corner, and a nightstand and lamp in another. She had just finished hanging her clothes in the little closet when she heard James call her name.

"Anna, come here, I want to show you something."

She stood next to James on the deck that faced the sparkling water with an arm around his waist, and he in turn wrapped an arm around her shoulder. The afternoon sun felt good on their bodies as James pointed in the direction of Lopez, Decatur, Shaw, Waldron, Stuart, and Orcas Islands. Friday Harbor hid behind Lopez Island, and to the east of Blakely, which they couldn't see, were Cypress, Guemes, Sinclair, and Lummi Islands.

Out on the water before them, motorboats and sailboats dotted the vast blueness. Anna breathed in the sweet scent of sun-warmed pine trees and the salt water that pushed against boulders that stood watch in the sand below the cliffs.

James heard Anna let out a heavy sigh.

"I know," he said, reading her mind. "It's always hard knowing that we have to leave—eventually."

"I don't even want to think about it, and I'm going to try not to."

James said reflectively, "You know, I was just thinking, in all the times I've been here, I really wish that the time had been spent with you."

Anna kissed James, and then before she could kiss him again he interrupted her.

"I suppose we should head down to the marina, because that's where the General Store is at, and we need to eat." With that decided they made their way in the cabin to find the key to the truck.

The white Chevrolet truck slowly traveled north along the narrow road, and even before they dipped down a short but steep hill, boats of every size could be seen through the trees. In the middle of the parking lot were gas pumps, and James wanted Anna to remind him, if he forgot, that out of courtesy, the gas tank need to be topped off before Wiley returned.

Along with their food purchases and a few bottles of wine, they left the store with a T-shirt and a coffee cup souvenir for Anna.

On the way back to the cabin, James asked Anna what she wanted to do first. Her answer did not surprise him. They packed a lunch, put the fishing tackle in the back of the truck and made their way up the crude dirt road to Trout Lake. Rocks poked out from the shaded, narrow, winding, and at spots slippery hill that was shared with an occasional motorcycle or a few hikers. At last the tired truck turned into a clearing and there was the lake that was described to her months ago.

"Oh, James," Anna sighed wistfully, "This is beyond wonderful."

Wiley's rowboat left the dock and headed around the lake. James mentioned that they would try to catch dinner after their lunch on the moss-covered rock. Anna was very quiet, and James understood. Her peaceful, glowing face spoke what words couldn't begin to explain.

While they ate sandwiches and sipped wine on the rock overlooking the rippling water, James told her that 60,000 fingerling trout are planted in the lake each year.

He explained, "In the morning, the holding tank truck is brought to the island. Trucks and jeeps arrive with buckets, and as soon as we hear the sound of the big truck, that's our signal to start the boat motors. We have to work fast, and as soon as the trout are scooped out, we dash across the lake and pour them in the water among the lake grass and lily pads. Everyone makes quite a few trips back and forth. It really gets the adrenaline going."

"How about if we try catching some of those trout?" Anna suggested.

The afternoon went by quickly and James asked Anna if the lake and its surroundings was everything she imagined it to be. There were little gushes of wind that made small whitecaps on the surface, and the sun warmed their backs while the colorful fishing lures twirled and spun in the water below.

Anna answered him by saying, "I have a new story to tell you. It's called, 'On the Lake'." She spoke quietly into the stillness:

"In the silence of the lake,
a bird's voice echoes across

the shimmering afternoon water.
In the silence that majestic trees create,
growing along, touching the water's edge,
sharing life with beautiful moss-covered boulders,
wind sweeps throughout branches
and my ears are filled with their song.
How old are the boulders
which hold back the rocky slopes above?
How old are the trees
that proudly surround the lake,
and the ones that have fallen
into the cool, deep, green water,
not wanting to be forgotten
at the depths where fish reside?
The tree thrusts upward,
a few branches basking in the warm sun.
And on the sparkling top of the lake,
a fish breaks the smooth surface;
a bug is caught, many circles made,
doubling and tripling in size until
nature ceases the rings.
The small bloop! the fish made
has silenced.
The first fishing pole I hold
which has been catching weeds so far,
has a different tug on it.
I overreact at the thought
of having caught a fish.
Not the kind that is wrapped
in plastic or sold frozen,
but the kind
that fights at the end of your line

Its silvery body emerges,
 breaking the surface as it flops around.
Out of the water
comes my first little fish.
Although he is small, he is larger
than the one my friend caught.
A picture is taken in the late afternoon sun,
with my small fish that just ate
the small bug."

At the cabin, after the trout was cleaned and put away until dinner, James took Anna down to the beach by way of a trail near the end of the runway. They walked hand in hand until an interesting rock, seashell, or hollow crab was spotted. Their footsteps wandered up and down the sloping sand banks. A ferry hummed in the distance. After a few hours of treading through the warm sand, they arrived at the other end of the runway and were thankful for solid ground.

On the way back to the cabin, Anna's footsteps were slowing. The sun was beginning to set and James suggested she take a short nap while he started a fire and prepared the barbecue.

She felt funny taking a nap before evening, so James practically had to steer her to her room and make sure she stretched out on the bed. Anna promised that she would have just a short rest, but while the trout were stuffed with onion, butter, and seasoning, James thought he heard snoring coming from her room. Peeking in on the sleeping occupant, he took an afghan that was at the end of the bed and carefully covered her curled up body. She looked so peaceful and pretty with her eyes closed. He couldn't help wonder if she was dreaming about her new adventures. It was going to be hard leaving the island since he knew how much it meant to her. James thought about kissing her on the cheek, but not wanting to take a chance of waking her, he crept out and softly shut the door.

The fish, he decided, could wait a little while longer, but the dark fireplace needed to be brought to life. James knew that Anna would love a warm, cozy fire after she awoke from her nap.

He gathered twigs and pinecones, along with an armload of split and seasoned firewood from the garage. In no time the wood began to crackle and pop, and the glow from the cheery fire softened and warmed the living room. When he was confident that the fire was going well and could survive for a while without him, James started on the rest of dinner. On the deck was a grill that was built from the same rock as the fireplace, and it was there that the trout were laid to cook.

James crossed his arms and stood on the edge of the deck, gazing west. The evening was cooling off and the bit of light was disappearing behind one of the islands. He did not want to feel envious for not having his own place on a private island where one could wander about, whether it was along the sandy shores or through the tree-covered hills leading to the two lakes. It was hard to keep such feelings from nagging at his heart, so he thanked God for his good friend Wiley for sharing the cabin with them.

Feeling a bit better, James turned his thoughts to what he and Anna could do the next day. There was another lake further down from the trout lake that was filled with bass. It didn't have the same character or beauty as the other lake, but it was still a nice place to explore.

There was a one-room log schoolhouse that still stood beside the main upper road. There were steep hills to climb that tightened leg muscles, covered ankles in dust, and tested one's stamina. They would have to dodge rocks, grab clumps of grass, and listen to a symphony of bugs urging them on. And upon reaching the top, the view of the San Juan Islands would be breathtaking.

His thoughts were interrupted by a soft voice behind him.

"James?"

She came up behind him and wrapped her arms around him.

"Feel better?"

"Yes, but I missed the sunset." Anna added, sounding a bit disappointed. "I wish you would have woken me up."

"Sorry, but when I checked on you, you were sleeping so peacefully that I didn't have the heart to wake you . . . just to cover you up with an afghan. Can I make it up to by serving you dinner and a glass of wine by the light of a fire?"

"That would be very nice—for starters."

James turned toward the kitchen. It was going to be a good evening.

~*~

"Anna," James quietly announced, "look out this window, but hold *real* still." James had been washing the breakfast dishes while Anna dried and put them away.

"Why?" She turned to look out the kitchen window, but did not expect to see two female deer cautiously grazing near the cabin.

"Oh, my Gosh! Am I really seeing, what I think I'm seeing?"

"Pretty, aren't they?"

"Why haven't we seen more of them?"

"They come down from the hills early in the morning while it's still quiet. When people start heading outdoors, they'll head back."

"Do you think we'll see more of them today?" she asked with yearning in her voice.

"Not likely." James shook his head. "Although they live in the forest, it's hard to spot them as they seem to disappear in the shadows." He suddenly thought of something else. "Say, after we're done, I want to get the morning paper at the store."

Anna wondered aloud if the cool morning air was any indication of what the rest of the day would be like. James shook his head and said that it should warm up nicely later on. With the kitchen clean and tidy, they set off in the old white truck whose heater was slow at warming. Although Anna wore her plaid jacket, driving through shady areas did not help her feel warm. The air at the marina was breezy and chillier than back at the cabin, and that's where Anna very much wanted to be— in front of a toasty fire drinking a cup of coffee.

Pulling into an unofficial parking spot that faced the south wall of the store, James hopped out of the truck, saying, "You stay here and try to keep warm. I'll be right back."

Anna crossed her arms under her chest and turned

her body slightly left on the bench seat so she could watch the sailboats bobbing in the choppy water. Her skin shivered and she wished James would hurry.

But something caught her eye.

James was standing near the front of the truck with the newspaper covering his chest. His hands that held the paper was putting a dent in the middle of it. James' face was very pale as shock dwelled in his eyes. He did not take his frightened stare off Anna as she slowly opened the passenger door, got out and came around to the front of the vehicle.

She stood before him and watched his eyes lower to the newspaper.

"James, what's wrong?" She tried to steady her shaking voice, and reaching out for the paper, Anna repeated his name, her tone turning insistent.

"James . . ."

Reluctantly, he handed it over to her, watching her face as she turned it right side up. It took a moment for her eyes to freeze, and then her face turned ashen gray. Anna leaned against the driver's side of the truck and James joined her.

"Well," Anna finally sighed after her color returned and the initial shock had passed. "Curly did say we were going to have a good harvest this year. He just didn't say it was going to be—early."

James was mystified. "Anna, what do crops have to do with her?"

She looked at the sailboats that gently rocked in the breeze, and a peaceful and content smile grew on her face while she lifted her chin. "I'm not speaking of crops, my dear friend. Fate has harvested a fool for me."

"A fool?" repeated James.

Anna let out a huff. "She was one, if she thought she could go on hurting people. Fate was looking out for me, and Life had had about enough of her too, I guess."

James and Anna got back in the truck, putting the paper between them and headed back to the cabin.

On the front page, a little place in Eastern, Washington made sensational headlines. The body of a plump, dark-haired woman wearing tight shoes was found hanged to death in her barn. It was yet unknown whether it was suicide or a homicide. The daughter and the husband were taken away for questioning, their lips stiff and their faces devoid of emotion.

Although, one of the officers had a different opinion that the others, saying that either way, it was irrelevant. "They looked as if a great burden had finally been lifted from their shoulders."

## CHAPTER 15—THE KILLDEERS' SONG

The late Sunday evening July sun shone on the Sports section of the paper sprawled over his legs that hung over the arm of his favorite chair

Somewhere, within the curvy and winding gray matter under his skull, his mother was reprimanding him for putting his legs on "her" chair, "her" this, or "her" that.

His legs stayed where they were.

Except for the occasional rustling of turning pages, the house was quiet and still. It was good that his mother lived a long distance away. When she did call, their conversation was strained and pulled like frayed thread on the verge of breaking. He did not particularly look forward to his mother's phone calls, for they were on his list of things he dreaded most. Every call was filled with words from a mother who was speaking to a thirteen-year-old boy instead of a man of thirty.

James put the paper down on his lap, intertwined

his fingers, and lay them to rest on his stomach while he explored the complexities of his relationship with his mother.

The warm and drowsy sun poured in from the south-facing window, uncovering swirling dust particles in the air. They were interesting little things to watch—interesting, like his mother.

At family gatherings, she told the world how her little Jimmy at the age of three, would vacuum dust bunnies from the air. Fortunately, Jimmy had since matured, and now being a young man of thirteen, he insisted on being called "James." Unfortunately, she neither saw nor wanted to understand that life carried on past the age of three in her only child.

The dust particles landed on tabletops, carpeting, bookshelves, the piano, and on himself. A very light layer gathered on the edges of the table beside him. Adorning the table were a week's worth of newspapers, a few books, and a stained plate with a fork settled among the few crumbs of what remained of Anna's blueberry pie.

He could almost hear his mother's voice calling, "Jimmy" . . .'

He could almost see her scolding finger wagging in front of his face after she gave his house the glove test. Before him stood Mother Edwards, her hands hiding somewhere within folds and layers of plump flesh where a waist once existed.

A cloud drew over the sun briefly and the room dimmed, and James shifted in the large chair, relieving his numb tailbone.

His mind was quick in its judgment. His feelings

for her were formed and decided before he could blink, and during the brief time before he blinked again, James was more than glad that she was a healthy distance from him.

It had been a long, long time since James could recall there every being a so-called mother-son relationship. The dust particles disappeared behind the curtain of the passing cloud, but certain memories could not be concealed by a cloud or forgotten by time itself. Certain memories lay beneath the crust of one's being; the wound, fresh and painful, was buried alive. Over time, the soil hardened, the grass grew, and life on went about its business. But the mother-son relationship had been buried below since his "rite of adolescence."

Engraved on the tombstone, if there had been one, the words would have read, "James Michael Edwards, Age 13, Buried Alive by his Mother."

It was during that birthday party that his mother started digging a grave in which she unknowingly would bury her relationship with her son.

It was going all right, for a party that was unwanted in the first place, for a boy of thirteen. The balloons and streamers suffocated the dining room, but were accepted. The announcement that cake and ice cream would be served before the opening of gifts was lukewarm in acceptance.

But the words that came out of her mouth after that severed her from her son. He wanted to disappear into the closest wall like Casper the Friendly Ghost or turn into a speck of dust and float into the fibers of the carpet.

"Now, boys, line up outside the washroom and

wash your hands," she instructed.

The stunned young men glanced stupidly at his mother and then at him, thinking this was surely all a joke. Seconds which were like hours to James pushed against the walls of silence and crushed him.

"Our what?" a guest boldly ventured to ask.

"Hands. Your hands!" Mother Edwards waved her own hands for emphasis. "Now go in and start washing," she repeated, "and no one gets one bite of cake and ice cream until they do!"

By now the young men shot their stares at James, wondering what kind of a wacky mother he had, and just what was he going to do about the situation.

"Jimmy, you first," she urged him, ushering him towards the bathroom. His face was hot; his numb body felt heavy like lead weighing him down to the floor. His reputation was at stake; his friends would laugh at him forever if he didn't do something quick.

"Come on guys! Let's go!" James led the pack down the hallway and to the front door.

"Jimmy, where are you going?" His mother's startled cry was barely audible behind them.

The front door was flung open and the pack of boys mounted their two-wheeled steeds and raced away with James in the lead. He glanced back only once to see his mother stomping her feet unceasingly upon the front lawn.

Her screams were heard blocks away. "Jimmy! Come back! Your cake—the ice cream is melting—the presents! Jimmy!"

That night, Mr. Edwards yelled at his wife while James listened from his upstairs bedroom.

"You did what? I would have done the same thing but I would had stayed away a week! You embarrassed the crap out of him! The poor kid! Stop treating him like he's three years old. You've got to stop this, or you'll regret it someday, if it's not too late already. Go up to his room and apologize!"

The knock at his door belonged to his father, which was no surprise. His father, again, apologized for his wife's behavior. His father had been right about a lot of things.

It was too late.

~*~

The newspaper was placed on the floor, and crossing his arms upon his chest, James leaned his head back and closed his eyes. His mind was tired and his eyes heavy. The early evening sun warmed his face as his body crept into a deep slumber.

He was in a semi-dusk room when his eyes opened.

They did not open against their will. James was sleeping soundly one minute, and found himself fully awake the next. He wondered if he had heard something in the house which might have awoke him so quickly.

He sat motionless, keeping his mind silent and his ears sharp. After almost a quarter of a minute went by, James let out a small sigh, stretched, and turned on one of the living room lights.

A smile came to his face as he thought of Anna's next visit, just a day away. He wondered what she was doing at home right about now. If he really wanted to, he could go to her house and spend more time with her instead of just thinking about her.

Their once-a-week porch visits had fallen away

months and months ago. But tomorrow was "their" day, and it was going to be one of the most special days of his life.

He rose from his chair and crossed the room to where the piano waited to be played. But it would have to wait until tomorrow.

On top of the old instrument was the velvet box that James picked up and nervously opened. Running his fingers over the simple gold band, his heart quickened as he rehearsed what he would say to Anna.

Twilight was approaching as daylight bowed gracefully away. The atmosphere was perfect, just as Anna loved it. The air was pleasant—not too warm, not too cool. A sweet aroma from the earth and the sky shared their ingredients to make a setting for romance.

It was all so perfect.

But the woman he loved more than anything in the whole world was not with him. He wanted her to be part of his life; and he part of hers. He wanted to hug her, to kiss her, and say "I'll love you forever, forever you are mine."

He did not want to keep such actions and thoughts trapped in his mind. And as he stood there, with the velvet box in his hand, he knew that tomorrow was too far away.

He put the velvet box in his pants pocket while he hurried into the kitchen and grabbed the truck keys. The house door slammed shut, rattling a few old windows, but they didn't mind. His truck door slammed shut, but it didn't mind either. The window was quickly rolled down and the wind pressed against his hair, pushing it back. His hands were tight on the steering wheel while his body leaned forward, urging his steed on.

His breathing quickened and his heart pounded within its domain. Knowing that he was just a short distance from his destination, his heart swelled and it made his flesh move, and in his thoughts he was already holding Anna's hand as they stood on her porch steps.

James could hear himself ask, "Will you be my wife?" He saw her smile, and then she would say, "I thought you would never ask."

And from behind curtains and windows, a mother and father cried in joy. Sisters and brothers smiled and sighed, "At last!" The fields about them waved their heads of grain in joy, and even the crickets sang in celebration. The heavens shone bright lights upon him as he reached a high rise in the road. But then the truck seemed to stop on its own, pausing long enough for the driver to see that the rays from heaven were four headlights.

A car, or what was left of it, rested upside down on McManus land.

Wild eyes were fixed on a truck.

Pain emerged from his chest as his heart was severely tightened into a small rock.

His body seemed to float out of the truck.

The sickness he felt in his stomach was separate from his own body. The pounding of a heart and the overwhelming nausea in his gut belonged to someone else. His body floated with motionless wings to the wreckage that lay on its side.

Rounding the tailgate, he saw a shoe lying on the asphalt and his heart and mind tore loose. She lay like a broken doll, sprawled out on the old country road, and slowly he sank down beside her.

Anna's eyes made their way to his face. "I was coming . . . to see you," she whispered weakly.

His eyes moved over her bloody body. He had to force himself to look at her face. As his mouth opened, his throat muscles tightened around the words, but he pushed them forward. "I was coming to see you . . . " he choked out.

In her hand she held an envelope that was wrinkled and covered with blood. Anna coughed and managed to whisper, "For you . . . read."

James started to shake, and he wanted to be sick, and he wanted to cry.

"*Read*," she coughed.

Carefully, he took the card from her fingers, took out the piece of paper with her writing on it and read:

At the end of a rainbow, you'll find a pot of gold.
At the end of a story, you'll find it's all been told.
But our love has a treasure our hearts can always spend;
and it has a story without any end.
At the end of a river the water stops its flow.
At the end of a highway there's no place you can go.
But just tell me you love me, and you are only mine,
and our love will go on
Till the end of time.
Till the End of Time.
(Earl Grant)

Anna's eyes sought his with a desperate light. "James, I'm scared. Tell me this isn't happening. Tell me that we're on your porch doing something. Tell me anything so I won't think about dying because I'm afraid, very afraid."

James whispered through his own unbearable pain, "Anna, don't talk . . ."

"Oh, James!" She gasped the air so quickly, that it was almost cruelly sucked from her lungs as she said his name. Then her eyes opened wide in indescribable astonishment.

"Oh, pretty, pretty! My angel is so bright and beautiful. She is smiling at me, James! James, can you see her? She is looking at you. Now she is smiling . . ."

"Anna, shh," he said brokenly, his eyes never leaving her face. Then his tears were released and while he sobbed in spasms, the salty water stung his face and fell onto the face of the woman he loved.

As it happened, he wiped his face and brushed off the tears on his pants. It was then that he felt it. James put his hand in his pocket, took out the little velvet case, opened it, and lifting out the gold ring he showed it to her. Her face was as beautiful as a doe's, her eyes soft and gentle. A little smile, as much as she could manage, appeared for the occasion. James gently took her left hand and slipped the ring on her finger.

"I love you, my little lady bug . . ."

"James, whatever you do after I'm gone, don't forget about us. Don't forget me . . . please don't forget about me. . ."

Her eyes, although looking at him, or at least in his direction, were slipping away somewhere else.

His body started shaking uncontrollably. Her body was pulled close to his, as if to transfer life from his body to hers, if it were at all possible.

By now, early evening had given itself up to dusk. And off in the fields, a bird flew away, its voice echoing, "Killdeer, killdeer, killdeer . . ."

## CHAPTER 16— *A MOTHER A MEMORY*

James slowly came to as one does when coming out of a fainting spell. His body seemed to levitate, and his prickly feeling body spun but didn't spin while a humming, buzzing sound hung over his head. He leaned his head back against the padded chair and tried to breathe, yet his breathing was too fast and he was starting to hear that buzzing sound again. "Slower James," he told himself, "slow, slow, slow, that's it, easy does it. Nice and slow. You can do it. You can do it."

As the dizziness eased, James became aware of cool sweat on his forehead, on the back of his neck, and over his hands, and strangely, it made him shiver in the warm stuffy house.

Pound, pound, pound, pound. His heart was hammering in his chest and James started to panic. Was he having a heart attack?

"Oh God, no! No, no, no!"

He forced himself to stop thinking long enough to feel what was going on inside his body.

"Okay, okay, okay . . ."

There wasn't any pain in his chest or left arm. James swallowed and let out a deep, slow breath. "Okay. What happened? What the *hell* just happened?"

James thought he should at least open his eyes, but they were already open. The space around him was black and dead quiet—except for the ticking of the kitchen clock—that wonderful kitchen clock.

"I can hear *that* so I know I'm not dead . . ." James spoke out loud and let out a huge sigh of relief.

And while James sat in his favorite chair in total blackness—at least he thought it was his chair—something in his gut was making its way up. His stomach was sick and he broke out in a sweat again, and cursing for what he knew was going to happen, James quickly reached out for the lamp and turned it on and ran for the bathroom.

Afterward, James went to his room, turned the nightstand light on and lay down on his bed, still sweating lightly and shaking. His eyes could only stare at the ceiling. Was he sick? Did he eat something bad? What the *hell* happened? James kept staring at the ceiling and he knew it was something else.

He threw his body forward and his mind and heart screamed, "Anna's dead! "

Swinging his legs over the side of the bed, James wanted to be sick again, but he forced his mind to make sense, to back up, to do *something* because—Anna just died in his arms . . . but he was at home. She was in an accident and died . . . yet he was on his bed. She

actually had seen her guardian angel and had said that
the angel was smiling at him. James shook his head and
covered his face with his shaking hands.

"Oh God! What's going on?" he loudly groaned. "I
was there!" James started to breathe fast again and he
began to feel fuzzy and queasy.

"Breathe, man, breathe!" he ordered himself.

His fixed his eyes on the door and spoke to it in a
shaky voice, "I was reading the newspaper. I woke up—
something *caused* me to wake up. I was driving to
Anna's house when—when I saw headlights. A car was
upside down in the wheat field. Anna was—"

James was going out of his mind, and thinking that
he was going to throw up again, made a run for the
bathroom. Thankfully he didn't, but he splashed cold
water on his face again and again. James tried to keep
how Anna had looked out of his crazy head. That cold
sweaty feeling was creeping over him again, and
although not a damn bit of any of this made a lick of
sense to him, maybe—maybe this was nature's way of
protecting him.

"Damn it!" James yelled, banging both fists on the
door. "I—WAS—THERE! Damn it, damn it, damn it!"

James began to cry, and as his tears were released,
he sobbed in spasms. The salty water stung his face and
fell onto his hands that were holding on to the bathroom
sink. As it happened, he wiped his face and brushed off
the tears on his pants. It was then that he remembered.
James put his hand in his pants pocket, but—there was
no little velvet case and no gold ring. The ring—*the
ring*. Where was the ring?

James stood next to his chair and remembered

crossing the room to where the piano waited to be played. The velvet box had been on top of the old instrument and James had picked it up and nervously opened it. His fingers had run over the simple gold and diamond ring, and his heart quickened as he clearly remembered rehearsing what he had planned to say to Anna.

But there was no velvet box on top of the piano.

James ran a hand through his hair and he wanted a beer in the worst way—just for the sake of calming him down. He made his way to the kitchen—not for a can of beer but to grab the keys to the truck.

The front door slammed which rattled a few old windows, and the truck door shut while tires spun and kicked up dust. The world ahead and beyond the truck was pitch black. Reaching for the headlight switch, James flicked it on. The cab was stuffy so he cranked down the window, and instantly the breeze hit his face. His hands were shaking terribly from the rush of adrenaline, and he was afraid that if he didn't tighten his grip on the steering wheel, he would accidentally let go of it.

Even though his heart pounded wildly in his chest James kept his breathing even so he wouldn't pass out. Knowing that he was just a short distance from his destination made his heart tighten and turned his flesh cold. The heavens were dark and silent as were the crickets, and upon reaching the high rise in the road, the only visible lights were those of his vehicle. James slowed the truck down and came to a stop. There were no tire marks on the asphalt, and as far as he could tell, a car hadn't plunged into the wheat field. And further still, if there had been an accident, he would have passed the remains of emergency flares littered on the road.

Upon the old country road there were only James, his truck, and beyond the sea of blackness were acres and acres of land. His heart and his mind seemed to suffer less at the growing thought that all this may have just been a terrible nightmare, which he was not wholly convinced that it was not.

As he sat in his truck in the middle of the road, a strange force was almost pulling at his insides, pulling his body forward so that James thought it best to obey. His truck instinctively knew where to turn along the dark country road, and making his way up the long driveway, James only saw blackness ahead of him. No warm, welcoming lights spilling onto the front lawn. No front door was open to cool off the house. Not even a single soft light spilled out from the barn. James took in the scene before him. It was dark, black, empty, death, and mournful—confusion and panic rose in him because he knew something had happened.

In a matter of a few moments his truck slid to a stop, narrowly missing the porch, and the door could not be opened fast enough. It hung open while the engine continued to run. James flung open the squeaky screen door and banged on the front door with all his might, and from within, bodies that had been perfectly asleep for hours awoke in panic and stumbled into the hallway.

The youngest sister cried, "Are we being robbed?"

"What! Robbers don't announce their intentions, stupid," snapped Gareth.

Anna emerged from her room with her eyes closed and she mumbled something about her sleep being disturbed.

"Richard, do you have the rifle?" Mrs. McManus asked in a panicked voice.

"Right here!" he replied in a brusque tone.

Mr. McManus cautiously made his way down the stairs, rifle pointed toward the floor.

Still, the loud and persistent banging continued, but then—they thought they heard a voice.

"Anna, Anna, are you there! Let me in! Let me in!" the voice cried.

"What the Sam Heck?" Richard rushed for the door, flicked on the porch light that somebody had forgotten to turn on, and the other switch lit the lamp in the foyer. Rushing in like a half-crazed man, James stood in the entryway looking like he had seen a ghost.

"James—what—what are you doing here?" Richard asked in a flabbergasted voice.

The young man could only stare wildly up the stairwell and began to rush toward it. "Where's Anna?" he cried. "Where is she?" he cried.

Keeping a hand about her lightweight robe as to keep it together at her chest, Polly came down the stairs keeping the other hand on the railing.

"James, dear—what on earth is the matter?" she wished to know.

The young man blinked, and quickly looked at Richard, then at Polly. Glancing up he saw Gareth, some sisters, and then another figure appeared. She was squinting her eyes and had a hand half-covering them.

James could not believe what he was seeing.

"Anna!"

The sleepy voice from above was reproachful as she gently scolded him, "James . . .why are you so loud?"

He slowly became aware that eyes—worried eyes—were upon him, and the dark veil of mystery was thinning. Anna was descending the stairs and she came to rest on the last riser.

In his insensibility to comprehend the breadth of his absurdity he murmured, "I don't understand . . ."

"Didn't you get enough of this family today?" Anna joked, slightly mocking, as she was still very groggy, stepping down to the foyer.

"But you were—oh, thank God!" He rushed at her and wrapped his arms tightly around her, pinning her arms to her side. "Oh, thank God! Oh, thank God!" he gasped and sighed in relief.

Anna was making a sniffing noise and then she remarked, "James . . . sweetie. . . what do I smell?" She leaned her head back and wrinkled her face. "James . . . what is that?"

"Huh?" He was still holding onto Anna tightly but sensed that she was trying to lean further away from his embrace.

"Did she just call him, 'sweetie'?" the youngest sister distastefully inquired.

Mrs. McManus threw a stern look at her daughter who stood at the top of the landing and said to her, "Enough of that. Now go to bed—all of you."

The sisters turned and the brothers disappeared without saying a word, but Gareth sat down on the top step of the landing, crossed his arms, and raised his eyebrows when his mother looked at him. She could only smile at her son while he winked back at her.

James slowly released Anna, but as he did he began to wobble and his knees felt very weak. Mr. McManus quickly leaned his rifle against a corner and started to summon Gareth, but the sound of bare feet was already scurrying down the stairs. Gareth squeezed in between Anna and James, supporting his left side, while Mr. McManus placed himself under James' right arm.

"Alright, let's get him over to the couch," Mr. McManus instructed.

The spent and exhausted young man who lay on the couch broke out in a thin layer of sweat as he mumbled nonsensical words into the early morning air—Anna's name being the exception. He was trying to explain, yet with each passing word his tired eyelids lowered, yielding to mental fatigue. Mrs. McManus brought a pillow and a lightweight blanket into the room, and with Gareth's help the pillow was placed under James' head, and she draped the blanket over him. She put her hand on James' forehead and let her motherly eyes ponder what her hand was feeling. She nodded her head and sighed. "Hmm, he does feel a bit warm."

A few minutes went by in near silence, that is, until Anna suppressed a yawn.

"What on earth do you think happened?" Mrs. McManus asked worriedly as she looked down on the handsome young man who was now fast asleep. "The poor dear boy . . . I think he'll be needing a shower in the morning after he gets up."

Mr. McManus slowly nodded his head in agreement, adding, "It's probably good that he fell asleep. He's in no shape to be driving back home."

"Oh, that reminds me," Mrs. McManus interjected with a request, "Dear, would you and Gareth mind driving over to his place right now? I would hate to think that appliances or something had been left on in his rush over here. And while you're there, go into his bedroom and get a change of clothes—find his shaver and toothbrush—everything."

While Mr. McManus stood in a sleepy daze, fully having heard his wife yet wanting to go back to bed instead of driving a short distance in the dark, he grinned, knowing, what he had to do.

"Thank you dear," his wife replied.

"We're on it. Let's go, dad—I'll drive," Gareth was saying, holding the front door open. Then he sputtered, "What! His truck is running. James didn't turn it off, and—he almost hit the house. Holy cow!"

"Um, Dad, Gareth—are you going out like that?" Anna casually pointed out.

"Huh?" the two men replied in one voice. Looking down at their summer sleepwear, they quietly laughed and Mr. McManus declared with a chuckle, "Oh. I suppose we should put something else on."

After the men drove off in James' truck, Anna's mom turned to her and suggested, "I think that it might be a good idea if you were to keep an eye on James. I wouldn't want him waking up and getting disoriented. How about if you go upstairs and bring your things down so you can sleep on the adjoining couch?"

~*~

Mrs. McManus sat quietly in the semi-dark room with James asleep on one couch and Anna asleep on the other. She had opened the front screen door to let the cool, early-morning air in the house. Her right leg was crossed over her left knee, and her right foot bounced slightly as she studied the sleeping young man. With her arms crossed and head tilting back and forth as she thought, Mrs. Manus just did not know what to make of it all.

James may have been in a deep sleep, but the woman who watched over him was very much awake, as many possibilities for his behavior swirled around in her head. All met with instant rejection, yet—as terribly fond as they were of James, what did they really know about him, other than him being the nephew of Pastor and Mrs. Edwards? She began to count in her head how many months it had been since her daughter had snuck out of the house to pay James an early morning visit a few months after his arrival.

In the following months, when the road began to smooth out for the two of them, James had demonstrated nothing but politeness, goodness, and an eagerness to please her eldest daughter. What about his temperament? As brief as his history was with their family, his temper had only been seen on a few occasions, and if the extent of his anger were only that of a particular Sunday service that lasted all of fifteen minutes, that was paltry evidence of an ill-temperament in her estimation.

She began to wonder about—other things. Things that families did not like to bring up or discuss. She and her husband had known Pastor and Mrs. Edwards for years, decades even, and they were surely both of sound mind. James' father, who had visited only briefly at Thanksgiving, seemed fine, not displaying any abnormal tendencies. Though, it could be said without argument that mental illness isn't worn like a noticeable scar on the skin. James had never spoken about his mother to anyone—even after the incident at the table during Thanksgiving. She wanted to know, of course, why James never mentioned her name, but she would not be the busybody mother of her daughter's best friend.

Mrs. McManus changed the position of her legs, crossing the left over the right. She let out a sigh and then yawned a slow, deep yawn. What was taking the men so long? She leaned her head back against the chair and a door slowly opened in her mind that recalled an event that happened decades ago on her side of the family.

Years ago, her great-grandmother's brother had burned down the family home in North Dakota. He had gone downstairs to feed the central furnace. Smoke soon filled the top floors and by the time it was noticed, it was too late to do anything about the fire. He had placed a tire in the furnace. That great uncle was mentally "unwell," as was another uncle on her side. He had been the one who had bought a small organ for her grandmother who had expressed an interest in playing one. Tragedy struck in a different form as that uncle hanged himself in the family barn. She remembered her father ordering the family to stay inside the house after he had made the discovery. Another tragic case of a mentally "unwell" person.

Polly was starting to drift off to sleep herself when she heard the sound of the truck coming toward the house.  Opening her eyes, she saw her husband coming in the house carrying clothes, with Gareth right behind him.

"Everything was fine," her husband whispered, putting the pile of clothes on the coffee table.  "Looks like things are better here, too.  Let's go back to bed—for a few hours."

"Sounds good," Polly agreed, taking her husband's hands that were being offered to her.

"See you both in a few—" Gareth yawned and then smiled, "hours."

When their son was several steps ahead of them, Mr. McManus bent his head toward his wife, and in a whisper divulged, "We came across a little velvet box hidden between James' T-shirts in his bedroom dresser drawer."

Mrs. McManus turned her head slightly toward her husband to see him wink, and in her tiredness she could only give a wry little grin and wink in return, as they continued up the stairs and to their room.

~*~

"Good morning," a male voice softly and hesitantly murmured.

"Well, good morning!" Mrs. McManus cheerfully smiled as she turned and took in the disoriented and disheveled young man who sheepishly stood just out of the kitchen.  The first thing that ran through her mind was, "The poor dear . . . he looks dreadful!"

James just stood there with a look on his unshaven face that sought a mother's pity and understanding—and even though she was not his mother, her heart and body instinctively went to him, holding his warm hands in hers, placing one on his forehead saying that he no longer had a slight fever.

Before James was allowed to feel any more awkward, Mrs. McManus smiled lovingly at him and said, "I know what you're thinking and I'll have none of it. Now, you go grab those clothes of yours and take a nice, long shower. I'll have coffee and breakfast waiting for you when you're done. Okay?"

"Okay." James' mouth lifted in a happy and agreeable way.

By the time James emerged from the bathroom, he was cleaned up and so was the kitchen, but the delicious aroma of bacon, eggs, hash browns, and toast lingered warmly in the air. Mrs. McManus saw him coming, and grabbing a towel, she opened the oven, took out a foil covered plate, and placed it on the table. James settled in the chair in front of his breakfast and scooted forward.

"I had the oven on warm so the plate shouldn't be too hot," she explained, while bringing silverware, a napkin, and coffee to James.

"Thank you," he offered, and still looking a bit sheepish, he bowed his head, folded his hands with fingers intertwined, and closed his eyes while he prayed:

"Heavenly Father, kind and good,
we thank Thee for our daily food.
We thank Thee for Thy love and care.
Be with us Lord, and hear our prayer."

"Amen! Now please eat," Mrs. McManus

requested of the young man. "I'll be outside hanging wash on the line, if you need me for anything."

James nodded his head and said he'd be out after he ate and washed his dishes.

~*~

The bright morning sun was still comfortable as the temperature had not risen yet, on what should be another fine, dry July day. Mrs. McManus greeted her old, dear friend the wash line with a courteous nod, and then proceeded to tie her clothespin apron bag around her middle. Although laundry was a never-ending chore, especially on a farm, she didn't mind it so much during the summer months as it allowed her be outside, where she preferred to be.

She had always enjoyed the pleasure of hanging wash in the sweet country air under the warmth of the sun, watching it flap in the breeze, and after the white sheets were dried and gleaming in the sun, there was a lovely, fresh smell to the sheets when you lay down at night.

As a wife and mother, there was always a flurry of busyness about her, but this gave her a few minutes of peace with her thoughts, and she prayed regularly for each person who wore the clothes as she hung them.

Her body was busy doing something routine and her mind was free to wander. Many of her early memories were of watching her mother and grandmother do the wash.

When autumn's cold rains finally put an end to outdoor drying, she would come across a piece of clothing at the bottom of her dresser, the clothespin marks still on the shoulders, and it still had the smell of having been dried outdoors. Her sense of smell was keen and strong memories surfaced from not long ago to decades past. Precious memories of her soft grandmother, or when her children were babies were all from recollections that the sweet country air reminded her of, and that alone was reason enough to make countless trips from the laundry room to the wash line worthwhile.

The sound of footsteps walking across the front porch caught her attention and brought her back from days of long ago.

"I don't think I've ever seen a person look so happy or content," James remarked as he came near.

Mrs. McManus smiled and asked if he had enough breakfast to last him a while. He said he had and he thanked her.

"May I help?" James asked.

"If you like." She paused. "Ever hung wash outside like this?"

"Can't say I have."

Mrs. McManus held up the end of a dish towel with her left hand and folded the corner back against the cord, reaching down in the pocket of her apron, taking out a wooden pin and squeezing it open over the corner and released the spring.

"Did your mother do this when you were younger?" she asked, hoping her gentle question would nudge a bit of information out of him.

James had been watching how Mrs. McManus worked the wooden pins and just how much of the garment or towel she folded on the line away from her. He wanted to try this new thing. After he was given a handful of the wooden pins, she suggested that perhaps he start with the socks.

Mrs. McManus thought James was evading or had forgotten her question, but he had not.

He let out a sigh and paused before he spoke. "I do not wish for you to think that my not sharing details about my mother is a sign of secrecy or disrespect toward you. I don't mean to keep things from you, it's just that—there isn't much to say that's worth sharing."

James reached down in the wicker basket for more socks. "If she had been anything like you—I'd be bragging all over the place."

Mrs. McManus smiled.

James pinned up a few more socks. "However, she has never given me a reason to do so." He cast a heavy sigh into the morning air. "She is a very complex woman. My vagueness toward my mother comes from her lack of ability to love, and the only thing that was— that *is* important in her life is herself."

Facing Mrs. McManus, James pinned up more socks, moving further down the line. "I wish my mother had done this. Growing up, I was envious of the other kids' mothers up and down our street, as they were always outside, visiting with the next-door neighbors."

"Envious? How so?" Mrs. McManus lightly asked, unaware that her hands had come to rest on the line.

James stopped what he was doing, and looking at the woman near him, let out another sigh. "This," he gestured with open arms toward the wash around him, "this had always been a sign to me that someone was home, that someone was looking after others, and that someone cared about the values of thrift."

The young man shook his head and looked down at the trodden lawn. He casually shrugged his shoulders and slowly concluded, "That's about it," with a short, shallow laugh.

James made a noise in his throat, and Mrs. McManus put a comforting hand on his arm and patted it. He made another throaty sound and tried to force a grin while nodding, which was followed by a short snuff, and as James slowly turned to leave, her loving hand slid down his arm and into his strong hand. Although he could not bring himself to look at her, he gave her hand a quick squeeze and then departed for home.

## CHAPTER 17—THE QUIET SYMPHONY OF LOVE

Another Day of the Lord was approaching, and while Anna was safely nestled way at the café, her parents and her companion spoke freely during the middle of the week. James explained to them what happened the Sunday before and needless to say his story shocked them, although it certainly explained his bizarre behavior. James was enlightened that he had woke the family around three in morning, and he was profoundly apologetic. All was forgiven, if there were anything to forgive.

James knew the harvest of both wheat and heart was ripe. Permission was granted by the father of the one he loved, adored, and could not live without. He had wished to be respectful of Anna's father and asked for his blessing on their union before taking the next step toward matrimony. It showed Anna's father that he was sincere in his intentions and this gesture was the mark of a true gentleman. James had always viewed it as an important tradition, a rite of passage, and a bonding experience between the groom-to-be and a future father-in-law.

~*~

The hills around him were formed several ice ages ago as glaciers advanced from the north, depositing glacial flour, and lakes were formed. Eventually they drained, leaving behind monumental quantities of silt. As time passed, prevailing winds blew the silt and dust around the region, forming giant sand dunes. Standing upon these hills among the waving grain, a young man knew that he had reached the end of his journey and wished to remain here for the rest of his days. He wanted everything that this way of life offered; he wanted Anna, he wanted her family, and he wanted the presence of her strong and steady parents. He wanted to be a better person, he wanted to be more involved with the community, and ultimately to be a better servant of God.

Those golden hills of ancient times, the rolling hills of tradition, the generations of the past now held in the earth's warm embrace; James felt like Abraham of the Bible when God told him that his descendants would be as numerous as the stars in the sky. Although he did not own this land, his soul did. He did not think the earth could ever pull and hold him down as it did now— and he did not fight it as he had before. He turned his face into the warm evening breeze and his cup of happiness and contentment overflowed to the point where it was incredibly unbelievable.

The young man knew that his body would never be buried in the city from which he had come. It did not matter—he did not care. A wonderful gust of wind hit him—this—his body, mind, and soul sang—*this*. This—the wind pushed against his chest and he raised his arms in instinctive celebration. The familiar wind caressed his face—this, he deeply sighed. He stood at an incline facing the crest of a dune-covered wheat field, and bowing and nodding toward him and around him were the musicians; God was the conductor and His mighty breath was the baton.

The young man cried, "God is great! God is good! He brings endless joy upon my soul! Where darkness had dwelled, light has filled my being. In my weakness, I have been made strong."

He heard the orchestra play its heart out, for the Conductor of Life had been rehearsing for this moment with the musicians, long ago, ever since he was a star in heaven.

An overwhelming banquet of love and joy stuck him, leaving him vulnerable to heaven and earth to nourish his spirit. It did not matter if he cried in front of the musicians; between himself and the land an unspoken pinnacle had been reached. The tears flowed and his body shook as he lowered himself onto the earth. The sun was blowing kisses on the horizon as it was setting behind the hills.

The older man who stood watching at the crest of the hill had seen and heard it all, and he understood. Backing away, he turned and made his way back to the farmhouse to await the younger man's return.

~*~

Sunday service had come and gone. James dined with the family for supper as he had done for months.

It was an ordinary Sunday with James, their church pastor, James, their sister's constant companion, and soon, their sister's fiancé.

Mr. McManus, Gareth, and the other brothers were busy with evening chores. Anna's mother had forgotten to take the laundry off the line, and so mother and daughter unfastened wooden pins from the line, neatly folded the dried clothes and placed them in the wicker basket. Once again the clothesline was empty and Anna's mother bowed to her friend, which always gave Anna a cause to chuckle. The women each grabbed an end of the heavy basket and made their way up the porch steps and into the house.

It was then that her mother announced that she couldn't remember if the eggs had been collected for the day. Anna offered to go, but her mother replied that she had not seen her feathered girls for the day, and she wished to bid them good night. Anna was instructed to put the laundry hamper in her own room, instead of her mother's room where the laundry was usually sorted. With that, her mother was gone. Anna stood there. The house was very quiet. Too quiet. Not a soul to be seen or heard. Anna sighed, then picked up the heavy basket and hauled it up the stairs.

Approaching her room, she was startled to see colors. As she entered her room she saw a cluster of red, pink, and white heart-shaped balloons tied to the end of her bed. Anna placed the laundry basket on the bed. Leaning against her pillow was an old-fashioned card and opening it, she read James' sweet handwriting that said, "Your violin has been kidnapped. Bring your heart as ransom."

She made haste to her window that faced the barn and she saw more balloons—red, pink, and white. Her heart took off, beating wildly out of her body. Anna began to dash out of her room but then she stopped, looked down at her clothes, and returned to her closet. She floated out of her room with her hair brushed and done up nicely, makeup touched up, and she had on the same pretty dress and heels she had worn to the Harvest Dance.

In the area from the house to the barn were large balloons with long strings attached to rocks. Written individually on those balloons were the sweetest, most wonderful words Anna had ever seen in her whole life. "Anna, McManus, will, you, make, me, the, happiest, man, on, earth, by, becoming, my, wife, for, life, PLEASE?"

In the field behind the barn, James Michael Edwards stood a short distance from his piano, dressed in the same handsome suit he had worn to the Harvest Dance. Anna's violin rested on top of the piano. He waited.

One by one, Anna followed the balloons and gathered them up. When she reached the edge of the barn and rounded the corner, all James could see was the bobbing of red, pink, and white balloons being carried by shapely arms and legs. The balloons came closer, and one by one, he watched them rise above the barn and up into the evening sky. His heart stopped and then swelled as he gazed at Anna. She slowly made her way over to him, smiling the most beautiful smile he had ever seen in his life. Her eyes lifted and took in the piano, and then she gave an unhurried nod—the kind of nod that meant a happy approval had been given. The young man who was so crazy in love with the most precious gift on earth stretched out his hand to her and, fixing her loving eyes on him, he led her to the piano at the edge of the wheat field.

James picked up a card that was on the piano and handed it to Anna. She took it, opened it, and read it out loud:

*"Till the End of Time"*

*At the end of a rainbow, you'll find a pot of gold.*
*At the end of a story, you'll find it's all been told.*
*But our love has a treasure our hearts can always spend;*
*and it has a story without any end.*
*At the end of a river the water stops its flow.*
*At the end of a highway there's no place you can go.*
*But just tell me you love me, and you are only mine, and*
*our love will go on till the end of time.*
*(Earl Grant)*

James did not speak, for there are some things which are far better understood without words. He put his hand in his pocket and brought forth the mint green velvet box and carefully opened it, for its hinges were of faded gold and it had seen a lifetime of leisure. The antique ring was asked to leave its furrowed home, and lifting out the century old treasure with trembling hands, James looked into Anna's eyes with the purest and deepest love imaginable.

Sunset is defined in astronomy as the moment when

the trailing edge of the sun's disk disappears below the horizon, casting hues of blushing, glowing, rosy pinks and tones of auburns, gingers, carrots and reds.

Nature was beckoning and swept a hand over the two hearts. A gentle breeze came off the rolling hills and played through the blades of tall dry grass, and in the nearby trees it caused leaves to sway. The late summer sky bent down to touch the hilltops of gold, and upon the faint breeze words were whispered to the trees.

What more must they do? But then they heard the young man ask, "Will you be my wife?"

And then, they saw her smile, for the young lady's senses were not blind, for she had heard the nudging of nature and replied in the faintest of sighs, "I thought you would never ask."

Her face was as beautiful as a doe, her eyes soft and gentle. A precious sweet smile, as much as she could manage without crying, appeared for the occasion.

He likewise had the same adoring gaze on his face, and lifting her hand, James carefully slipped the ring on her finger. He proceeded to tenderly kiss the top of her hand and the palm of her hand, and then he kissed her forehead where his lips lingered.

On the sweet August evening breeze, his voice whispered gently beside her ear to say, "I love you, my little lady bug."

Turning towards the piano, he opened the violin case and ceremoniously handed the instrument to Anna, then sat down at the piano. Their song was played as if they were one, with a shared heart, mind, and soul as the music drifted up into the heavens that had long awaited their union.

From behind her bedroom window and curtains, the jar of memories that held the harvest moon wept with happiness, and from within the old barn, peering out from cracks in the cedar walls, a mother and father quietly shared their own tears, along with sisters and brothers who smiled and sighed, "At last!" The fields about them waved their tops of grain in joy, and even the crickets sang in celebration.

By now, early evening had given itself up to twilight.

And off in the fields, somewhere, a bird flew away, its voice softly echoing, "Killdeer, killdeer, killdeer. . ." until its song faded down the fields and into the darkness beyond.

*~THE END~*

"Thank you for reading THE KILLDEER SONG. Gaining exposure as an independent author relies mostly on word-of-mouth, so if you have the time and inclination, please consider leaving a short review wherever you can."

Thank you,
*Margie Bayer*

## About the Author

Margie Bayer lives in Auburn, Washington with her husband and two sons.

Her hobbies include writing novels, gardening, growing dahlias, genealogy, and amateur photography.

You can find Margie Bayer at:

On the author's Facebook page at
www.facebook.com/margiebayer.author

Margie Bayer at www.amazon.com and Barnes and Noble.com where E-Book and Paperback is available.

Pinterest at www.pinterest.com/bayer0830 where she has storyboards for her novels.

Proof

Made in the USA
Charleston, SC
24 May 2016